Four Max Carrados Detective Stories by Ernest Bramah

Ernest Bramah was born on 20th March 1868. He was an intensely private man and very little about his life was ever released.

Bramah dropped out of Manchester Grammar school at sixteen, in almost all his subjects he was close to the bottom of his class, and took a job at a farm. His father then invested substantial sums in setting him up with his own farm but Bramah's long term interests were elsewhere. In his spare time he would write vignettes on local subjects and send them to The Birmingham News for publication.

In a now rather dramatic change of career he obtained the position of secretary to Jerome K Jerome and then to editing one of Jerome's magazines. Thereafter Bramah edited journals for a publishing firm that only ceased with its bankruptcy.

He obtained success in his own right with the creation of the storyteller Kai Lung with humourous tales set in China, usually laced with fantasy elements. There seems to have been a certain vogue for stories with an oriental element at this time which Bramah was happy to take advantage of.

His career blossomed across many genres; in humour, science-fiction, and supernatural he was ranked with the very best of the day. Even Orwell cited his work as an influence and as a predictor for the rise of Fascism and his own novel, 1984.

At a time when the English Channel had yet to be crossed by an aeroplane, Bramah foresaw aerial express trains traveling at 10,000 feet, a nationwide wireless-telegraphy network, fax machines and cypher writing typewriters similar to the German Enigma machine.

In 1914, Bramah created the blind detective Max Carrados. Despite the obvious obstacle to his deductive powers he was a literary and commercial success.

Ernest Bramah died in Weston-Super-Mare on 27th June 1942 at the age of 74.

Index of Contents

THE COIN OF DIONYSIUS

It was eight o'clock at night and raining, scarcely a time when a business so limited in its clientele as that of a coin dealer could hope to attract any customer, but a light was still showing in the small shop that bore over its window the name of Baxter, and in the even smaller office at the back the proprietor himself sat reading the latest Pall Mall. His enterprise seemed to be justified, for presently the door bell gave its announcement, and throwing down his paper Mr. Baxter went forward.

As a matter of fact the dealer had been expecting someone and his manner as he passed into the shop was unmistakably suggestive of a caller of importance. But at the first glance towards his visitor the excess of deference melted out of his bearing, leaving the urbane, self-possessed shopman in the presence of the casual customer.

"Mr. Baxter, I think?" said the latter. He had laid aside his dripping umbrella and was unbuttoning overcoat and coat to reach an inner pocket. "You hardly remember me, I suppose? Mr. Carlyle—two years ago I took up a case for you—"

"To be sure. Mr. Carlyle, the private detective—"

"Inquiry agent," corrected Mr. Carlyle precisely.

"Well," smiled Mr. Baxter, "for that matter I am a coin dealer and not an antiquarian or a numismatist. Is there anything in that way that I can do for you?"

"Yes," replied his visitor; "it is my turn to consult you." He had taken a small wash-leather bag from the inner pocket and now turned something carefully out upon the counter. "What can you tell me about that?"

The dealer gave the coin a moment's scrutiny.

"There is no question about this," he replied. "It is a Sicilian tetradrachm of Dionysius."

"Yes, I know that—I have it on the label out of the cabinet. I can tell you further that it's supposed to be one that Lord Seastoke gave two hundred and fifty pounds for at the Brice sale in '94."

"It seems to me that you can tell me more about it than I can tell you," remarked Mr. Baxter. "What is it that you really want to know?"

"I want to know," replied Mr. Carlyle, "whether it is genuine or not."

"Has any doubt been cast upon it?"

"Certain circumstances raised a suspicion—that is all."

The dealer took another look at the tetradrachm through his magnifying glass, holding it by the edge with the careful touch of an expert. Then he shook his head slowly in a confession of ignorance.

"Of course I could make a guess—"

"No, don't," interrupted Mr. Carlyle hastily. "An arrest hangs on it and nothing short of certainty is any good to me."

"Is that so, Mr. Carlyle?" said Mr. Baxter, with increased interest. "Well, to be quite candid, the thing is out of my line. Now if it was a rare Saxon penny or a doubtful noble I'd stake my reputation on my opinion, but I do very little in the classical series."

Mr. Carlyle did not attempt to conceal his disappointment as he returned the coin to the bag and replaced the bag in the inner pocket.

"I had been relying on you," he grumbled reproachfully. "Where on earth am I to go now?"

"There is always the British Museum."

"Ah, to be sure, thanks. But will anyone who can tell me be there now?"

"Now? No fear!" replied Mr. Baxter. "Go round in the morning—"

"But I must know to-night," explained the visitor, reduced to despair again. "To-morrow will be too late for the purpose."

Mr. Baxter did not hold out much encouragement in the circumstances.

"You can scarcely expect to find anyone at business now," he remarked. "I should have been gone these two hours myself only I happened to have an appointment with an American millionaire who fixed his own time." Something indistinguishable from a wink slid off Mr. Baxter's right eye. "Offmunson he's called, and a bright young pedigree-hunter has traced his descent from Offa, King of Mercia. So he—quite naturally—wants a set of Offas as a sort of collateral proof."

"Very interesting," murmured Mr. Carlyle, fidgeting with his watch. "I should love an hour's chat with you about your millionaire customers—some other time. Just now—look here, Baxter, can't you give me a line of introduction to some dealer in this sort of thing who happens to live in town? You must know dozens of experts."

"Why, bless my soul, Mr. Carlyle, I don't know a man of them away from his business," said Mr. Baxter, staring. "They may live in Park Lane or they may live in Petticoat Lane for all I know. Besides, there aren't so many experts as you seem to imagine. And the two best will very likely quarrel over it. You've had to do with 'expert witnesses,' I suppose?"

"I don't want a witness; there will be no need to give evidence. All I want is an absolutely authoritative pronouncement that I can act on. Is there no one who can really say whether the thing is genuine or not?"

Mr. Baxter's meaning silence became cynical in its implication as he continued to look at his visitor across the counter. Then he relaxed.

"Stay a bit; there is a man—an amateur—I remember hearing wonderful things about some time ago. They say he really does know."

"There you are," explained Mr. Carlyle, much relieved. "There always is someone. Who is he?"

"Funny name," replied Baxter. "Something Wynn or Wynn something." He craned his neck to catch sight of an important motor-car that was drawing to the kerb before his window. "Wynn Carrados! You'll excuse me now, Mr. Carlyle, won't you? This looks like Mr. Offmunson."

Mr. Carlyle hastily scribbled the name down on his cuff.

"Wynn Carrados, right. Where does he live?"

"Haven't the remotest idea," replied Baxter, referring the arrangement of his tie to the judgment of the wall mirror. "I have never seen the man myself. Now, Mr. Carlyle, I'm sorry I can't do any more for you. You won't mind, will you?"

Mr. Carlyle could not pretend to misunderstand. He enjoyed the distinction of holding open the door for the transatlantic representative of the line of Offa as he went out, and then made his way through the muddy streets back to his office. There was only one way of tracing a private individual at such short notice—through the pages of the directories, and the gentleman did not flatter himself by a very high estimate of his chances.

Fortune favoured him, however. He very soon discovered a Wynn Carrados living at Richmond, and, better still, further search failed to unearth another. There was, apparently, only one householder at all events of that name in the neighbourhood of London. He jotted down the address and set out for Richmond.

The house was some distance from the station, Mr. Carlyle learned. He took a taxicab and drove, dismissing the vehicle at the gate. He prided himself on his power of observation and the accuracy of his deductions which resulted from it—a detail of his business. "It's nothing more than using one's eyes and putting two and two together," he would modestly declare, when he wished to be deprecatory rather than impressive. By the time he had reached the front door of "The Turrets" he had formed some opinion of the position and tastes of the people who lived there.

A man-servant admitted Mr. Carlyle and took his card—his private card, with the bare request for an interview that would not detain Mr. Carrados for ten minutes. Luck still favoured him; Mr. Carrados was at home and would see him at once. The servant, the hall through which they passed, and the room into which he was shown, all contributed something to the deductions which the quietly observant gentleman was half unconsciously recording.

"Mr. Carlyle," announced the servant.

The room was a library or study. The only occupant, a man of about Carlyle's own age, had been using a typewriter up to the moment of his visitor's entrance. He now turned and stood up with an expression of formal courtesy.

"It's very good of you to see me at this hour," apologised Mr. Carlyle.

The conventional expression of Mr. Carrados's face changed a little.

"Surely my man has got your name wrong?" he explained. "Isn't it Louis Calling?"

Mr. Carlyle stopped short and his agreeable smile gave place to a sudden flash of anger or annoyance.

"No sir," he replied stiffly. "My name is on the card which you have before you."

"I beg your pardon," said Mr. Carrados, with perfect good-humour. "I hadn't seen it. But I used to know a Calling some years ago—at St. Michael's."

"St. Michael's!" Mr. Carlyle's features underwent another change, no less instant and sweeping than before. "St. Michael's! Wynn Carrados? Good heavens! it isn't Max Wynn—old 'Winning' Wynn"?

"A little older and a little fatter—yes," replied Carrados. "I have changed my name you see."

"Extraordinary thing meeting like this," said his visitor, dropping into a chair and staring hard at Mr. Carrados. "I have changed more than my name. How did you recognize me?"

"The voice," replied Carrados. "It took me back to that little smoke-dried attic den of yours where we—"

"My God!" exclaimed Carlyle bitterly, "don't remind me of what we were going to do in those days." He looked round the well-furnished, handsome room and recalled the other signs of wealth that he had noticed. "At all events, you seem fairly comfortable, Wynn."

"I am alternately envied and pitied," replied Carrados, with a placid tolerance of circumstance that seemed characteristic of him. "Still, as you say, I am fairly comfortable."

"Envied, I can understand. But why are you pitied?"

"Because I am blind," was the tranquil reply.

"Blind!" exclaimed Mr. Carlyle, using his own eyes superlatively. "Do you mean—literally blind?"

"Literally.... I was riding along a bridle-path through a wood about a dozen years ago with a friend. He was in front. At one point a twig sprang back—you know how easily a thing like that happens. It just flicked my eye—nothing to think twice about."

"And that blinded you?"

"Yes, ultimately. It's called amaurosis."

"I can scarcely believe it. You seem so sure and self-reliant. Your eyes are full of expression—only a little quieter than they used to be. I believe you were typing when I came....Aren't you having me?"

"You miss the dog and the stick?" smiled Carrados. "No; it's a fact."

"What an awful affliction for you, Max. You were always such an impulsive, reckless sort of fellow— never quiet. You must miss such a fearful lot."

"Has anyone else recognized you?" asked Carrados quietly.

"Ah, that was the voice, you said," replied Carlyle.

"Yes; but other people heard the voice as well. Only I had no blundering, self-confident eyes to be hoodwinked."

"That's a rum way of putting it," said Carlyle. "Are your ears never hoodwinked, may I ask?"

"Not now. Nor my fingers. Nor any of my other senses that have to look out for themselves."

"Well, well," murmured Mr. Carlyle, cut short in his sympathetic emotions. "I'm glad you take it so well. Of course, if you find it an advantage to be blind, old man—" He stopped and reddened. "I beg your pardon," he concluded stiffly.

"Not an advantage perhaps," replied the other thoughtfully. "Still it has compensations that one might not think of. A new world to explore, new experiences, new powers awakening; strange new perceptions; life in the fourth dimension. But why do you beg my pardon, Louis?"

"I am an ex-solicitor, struck off in connexion with the falsifying of a trust account, Mr. Carrados," replied Carlyle, rising.

"Sit down, Louis," said Carrados suavely. His face, even his incredibly living eyes, beamed placid good-nature. "The chair on which you will sit, the roof above you, all the comfortable surroundings to which you have so amiably alluded, are the direct result of falsifying a trust account. But do I call you 'Mr. Carlyle' in consequence? Certainly not, Louis."

"I did not falsify the account," cried Carlyle hotly. He sat down however, and added more quietly: "But why do I tell you all this? I have never spoken of it before."

"Blindness invites confidence," replied Carrados. "We are out of the running—human rivalry ceases to exist. Besides, why shouldn't you? In my case the account was falsified."

"Of course that's all bunkum, Max" commented Carlyle. "Still, I appreciate your motive."

"Practically everything I possess was left to me by an American cousin, on the condition that I took the name of Carrados. He made his fortune by an ingenious conspiracy of doctoring the crop reports and unloading favourably in consequence. And I need hardly remind you that the receiver is equally guilty with the thief."

"But twice as safe. I know something of that, Max ... Have you any idea what my business is?"

"You shall tell me," replied Carrados.

"I run a private inquiry agency. When I lost my profession I had to do something for a living. This occurred. I dropped my name, changed my appearance and opened an office. I knew the legal side down to the ground and I got a retired Scotland Yard man to organize the outside work."

"Excellent!" cried Carrados. "Do you unearth many murders?"

"No," admitted Mr. Carlyle; "our business lies mostly on the conventional lines among divorce and defalcation."

"That's a pity," remarked Carrados. "Do you know, Louis, I always had a secret ambition to be a detective myself. I have even thought lately that I might still be able to do something at it if the chance came my way. That makes you smile?"

"Well, certainly, the idea—"

"Yes, the idea of a blind detective—the blind tracking the alert—"

"Of course, as you say, certain facilities are no doubt quickened," Mr. Carlyle hastened to add considerately, "but, seriously, with the exception of an artist, I don't suppose there is any man who is more utterly dependent on his eyes."

Whatever opinion Carrados might have held privately, his genial exterior did not betray a shadow of dissent. For a full minute he continued to smoke as though he derived an actual visual enjoyment from the blue sprays that travelled and dispersed across the room. He had already placed before his visitor a box containing cigars of a brand which that gentleman keenly appreciated but generally regarded as unattainable, and the matter-of-fact ease and certainty with which the blind man had brought the box and put it before him had sent a questioning flicker through Carlyle's mind.

"You used to be rather fond of art yourself, Louis," he remarked presently. "Give me your opinion of my latest purchase—the bronze lion on the cabinet there." Then, as Carlyle's gaze went about the room, he added quickly: "No, not that cabinet—the one on your left."

Carlyle shot a sharp glance at his host as he got up, but Carrados's expression was merely benignly complacent. Then he strolled across to the figure.

"Very nice," he admitted. "Late Flemish, isn't it?"

"No, It is a copy of Vidal's 'Roaring Lion.'"

"Vidal?"

"A French artist." The voice became indescribably flat. "He, also, had the misfortune to be blind, by the way."

"You old humbug, Max!" shrieked Carlyle, "you've been thinking that out for the last five minutes." Then the unfortunate man bit his lip and turned his back towards his host.

"Do you remember how we used to pile it up on that obtuse ass Sanders, and then roast him?" asked Carrados, ignoring the half-smothered exclamation with which the other man had recalled himself.

"Yes," replied Carlyle quietly. "This is very good," he continued, addressing himself to the bronze again. "How ever did he do it?"

"With his hands."

"Naturally. But, I mean, how did he study his model?"

"Also with his hands. He called it 'seeing near.'"

"Even with a lion—handled it?"

"In such cases he required the services of a keeper, who brought the animal to bay while Vidal exercised his own particular gifts ... You don't feel inclined to put me on the track of a mystery, Louis?"

Unable to regard this request as anything but one of old Max's unquenchable pleasantries, Mr. Carlyle was on the point of making a suitable reply when a sudden thought caused him to smile knowingly. Up to that point, he had, indeed, completely forgotten the object of his visit. Now that he remembered the doubtful Dionysius and Baxter's recommendation he immediately assumed that some mistake had been made. Either Max was not the Wynn Carrados he had been seeking or else the dealer had been misinformed; for although his host was wonderfully expert in the face of his misfortune, it was inconceivable that he could decide the genuineness of a coin without seeing it. The opportunity seemed a good one of getting even with Carrados by taking him at his word.

"Yes," he accordingly replied, with crisp deliberation, as he re-crossed the room; "yes, I will, Max. Here is the clue to what seems to be a rather remarkable fraud." He put the tetradrachm into his host's hand. "What do you make of it?"

For a few seconds Carrados handled the piece with the delicate manipulation of his finger-tips while Carlyle looked on with a self-appreciative grin. Then with equal gravity the blind man weighed the coin in the balance of his hand. Finally he touched it with his tongue.

"Well?" demanded the other.

"Of course I have not much to go on, and if I was more fully in your confidence I might come to another conclusion—"

"Yes, yes," interposed Carlyle, with amused encouragement.

"Then I should advise you to arrest the parlourmaid, Nina Brun, communicate with the police authorities of Padua for particulars of the career of Helene Brunesi, and suggest to Lord Seastoke that he should return to London to see what further depredations have been made in his cabinet."

Mr. Carlyle's groping hand sought and found a chair, on to which he dropped blankly. His eyes were unable to detach themselves for a single moment from the very ordinary spectacle of Mr. Carrados's mildly benevolent face, while the sterilized ghost of his now forgotten amusement still lingered about his features.

"Good heavens!" he managed to articulate, "how do you know?"

"Isn't that what you wanted of me?" asked Carrados suavely.

"Don't humbug, Max," said Carlyle severely. "This is no joke." An undefined mistrust of his own powers suddenly possessed him in the presence of this mystery. "How do you come to know of Nina Brun and Lord Seastoke?"

"You are a detective, Louis," replied Carrados. "How does one know these things? By using one's eyes and putting two and two together."

Carlyle groaned and flung out an arm petulantly.

"Is it all bunkum, Max? Do you really see all the time—though that doesn't go very far towards explaining it."

"Like Vidal, I see very well—at close quarters," replied Carrados, lightly running a forefinger along the inscription on the tetradrachm. "For longer range I keep another pair of eyes. Would you like to test them?"

Mr. Carlyle's assent was not very gracious; it was, in fact, faintly sulky. He was suffering the annoyance of feeling distinctly unimpressive in his own department; but he was also curious.

"The bell is just behind you, if you don't mind," said his host. "Parkinson will appear. You might take note of him while he is in."

The man who had admitted Mr. Carlyle proved to be Parkinson.

"This gentleman is Mr. Carlyle, Parkinson," explained Carrados the moment the man entered. "You will remember him for the future?"

Parkinson's apologetic eye swept the visitor from head to foot, but so lightly and swiftly that it conveyed to that gentleman the comparison of being very deftly dusted.

"I will endeavour to do so, sir," replied Parkinson, turning again to his master.

"I shall be at home to Mr. Carlyle whenever he calls. That is all."

"Very well, sir."

"Now, Louis," remarked Mr. Carrados briskly, when the door had closed again, "you have had a good opportunity of studying Parkinson. What is he like?"

"In what way?"

"I mean as a matter of description. I am a blind man—I haven't seen my servant for twelve years—what idea can you give me of him? I asked you to notice."

"I know you did, but your Parkinson is the sort of man who has very little about him to describe. He is the embodiment of the ordinary. His height is about average—"

"Five feet nine," murmured Carrados. "Slightly above the mean."

"Scarcely noticeably so. Clean-shaven. Medium brown hair. No particularly marked features. Dark eyes. Good teeth."

"False," interposed Carrados. "The teeth—not the statement."

"Possibly," admitted Mr. Carlyle. "I am not a dental expert and I had no opportunity of examining Mr. Parkinson's mouth in detail. But what is the drift of all this?"

"His clothes?"

"Oh, just the ordinary evening dress of a valet. There is not much room for variety in that."

"You noticed, in fact, nothing special by which Parkinson could be identified?"

"Well, he wore an unusually broad gold ring on the little finger of the left hand."

"But that is removable. And yet Parkinson has an ineradicable mole—a small one, I admit—on his chin. And you a human sleuth-hound. Oh, Louis!"

"At all events," retorted Carlyle, writhing a little under this good-humoured satire, although it was easy enough to see in it Carrados's affectionate intention—"at all events, I dare say I can give as good a description of Parkinson as he can give of me."

"That is what we are going to test. Ring the bell again."

"Seriously?"

"Quite. I am trying my eyes against yours. If I can't give you fifty out of a hundred I'll renounce my private detectorial ambition for ever."

"It isn't quite the same," objected Carlyle, but he rang the bell.

"Come in and close the door, Parkinson," said Carrados when the man appeared. "Don't look at Mr. Carlyle again—in fact, you had better stand with your back towards him, he won't mind. Now describe to me his appearance as you observed it."

Parkinson tendered his respectful apologies to Mr. Carlyle for the liberty he was compelled to take, by the deferential quality of his voice.

"Mr. Carlyle, sir, wears patent leather boots of about size seven and very little used. There are five buttons, but on the left boot one button—the third up—is missing, leaving loose threads and not the more usual metal fastener. Mr. Carlyle's trousers, sir, are of a dark material, a dark grey line of about a quarter of an inch width on a darker ground. The bottoms are turned permanently up and are, just now, a little muddy, if I may say so."

"Very muddy," interposed Mr. Carlyle generously. "It is a wet night, Parkinson."

"Yes, sir; very unpleasant weather. If you will allow me, sir, I will brush you in the hall. The mud is dry now, I notice. Then, sir," continued Parkinson, reverting to the business in hand, "there are dark green cashmere hose. A curb-pattern key-chain passes into the left-hand trouser pocket."

From the visitor's nether garments the photographic-eyed Parkinson proceeded to higher ground, and with increasing wonder Mr. Carlyle listened to the faithful catalogue of his possessions. His fetter-and-link albert of gold and platinum was minutely described. His spotted blue ascot, with its gentlemanly pearl scarfpin, was set forth, and the fact that the buttonhole in the left lapel of his morning coat showed signs of use was duly noted. What Parkinson saw he recorded, but he made no deductions. A handkerchief carried in the cuff of the right sleeve was simply that to him and not an indication that Mr. Carlyle was, indeed, left-handed.

But a more delicate part of Parkinson's undertaking remained. He approached it with a double cough.

"As regards Mr. Carlyle's personal appearance, sir—"

"No, enough!" cried the gentleman concerned hastily. "I am more than satisfied. You are a keen observer, Parkinson."

"I have trained myself to suit my master's requirements, sir," replied the man. He looked towards Mr. Carrados, received a nod and withdrew.

Mr. Carlyle was the first to speak.

"That man of yours would be worth five pounds a week to me, Max," he remarked thoughtfully. "But, of course—"

"I don't think that he would take it," replied Carrados, in a voice of equally detached speculation. "He suits me very well. But you have the chance of using his services—indirectly."

"You still mean that—seriously?"

"I notice in you a chronic disinclination to take me seriously, Louis. It is really—to an Englishman—almost painful. Is there something inherently comic about me or the atmosphere of The Turrets?"

"No, my friend," replied Mr. Carlyle, "but there is something essentially prosperous. That is what points to the improbable. Now what is it?"

"It might be merely a whim, but it is more than that," replied Carrados. "It is, well, partly vanity, partly ennui, partly"—certainly there was something more nearly tragic in his voice than comic now—"partly hope."

Mr. Carlyle was too tactful to pursue the subject.

"Those are three tolerable motives," he acquiesced. "I'll do anything you want, Max, on one condition."

"Agreed. And it is?"

"That you tell me how you knew so much of this affair." He tapped the silver coin which lay on the table near them. "I am not easily flabbergasted," he added.

"You won't believe that there is nothing to explain—that it was purely second-sight?"

"No," replied Carlyle tersely: "I won't."

"You are quite right. And yet the thing is very simple."

"They always are—when you know," soliloquised the other. "That's what makes them so confoundedly difficult when you don't."

"Here is this one then. In Padua, which seems to be regaining its old reputation as the birthplace of spurious antiques, by the way, there lives an ingenious craftsman named Pietro Stelli. This simple soul, who possesses a talent not inferior to that of Cavino at his best, has for many years turned his hand to the not unprofitable occupation of forging rare Greek and Roman coins. As a collector and student of certain Greek colonials and a specialist in forgeries I have been familiar with Stelli's workmanship for years. Latterly he seems to have come under the influence of an international crook called—at the moment—Dompierre, who soon saw a way of utilizing Stelli's genius on a royal scale. Helene Brunesi, who in private life is—and really is, I believe—Madame Dompierre, readily lent her services to the enterprise."

"Quite so," nodded Mr. Carlyle, as his host paused.

"You see the whole sequence, of course?"

"Not exactly—not in detail," confessed Mr. Carlyle.

"Dompierre's idea was to gain access to some of the most celebrated cabinets of Europe and substitute Stelli's fabrications for the genuine coins. The princely collection of rarities that he would thus amass might be difficult to dispose of safely, but I have no doubt that he had matured his plans. Helene, in the person of Nina Brun, an Anglicised French parlourmaid—a part which she fills to perfection—was to obtain wax impressions of the most valuable pieces and to make the exchange when the counterfeits reached her. In this way it was obviously hoped that the fraud would not come to light until long after the real coins had been sold, and I gather that she has already done her work successfully in general houses. Then, impressed by her excellent references and capable manner, my housekeeper engaged her, and for a few weeks she went about her duties here. It was fatal to this detail of the scheme, however, that I have the misfortune to be blind. I am told that Helene has so innocently angelic a face as to disarm suspicion, but I was incapable of being impressed and that good material was thrown away. But one morning my material fingers—which, of course, knew nothing of Helene's angelic face— discovered an unfamiliar touch about the surface of my favourite Euclideas, and, although there was doubtless nothing to be seen, my critical sense of smell reported that wax had been recently pressed against it. I began to make discreet inquiries and in the meantime my cabinets went to the local bank for safety. Helene countered by receiving a telegram from Angiers, calling her to the death-bed of her aged mother. The aged mother succumbed; duty compelled Helene to remain at the side of her stricken patriarchal father, and doubtless The Turrets was written off the syndicate's operations as a bad debt."

"Very interesting," admitted Mr. Carlyle; "but at the risk of seeming obtuse"—his manner had become delicately chastened—"I must say that I fail to trace the inevitable connexion between Nina Brun and this particular forgery—assuming that it is a forgery."

"Set your mind at rest about that, Louis," replied Carrados. "It is a forgery, and it is a forgery that none but Pietro Stelli could have achieved. That is the essential connexion. Of course, there are accessories. A private detective coming urgently to see me with a notable tetradrachm in his pocket, which he announces to be the clue to a remarkable fraud—well, really, Louis, one scarcely needs to be blind to see through that."

"And Lord Seastoke? I suppose you happened to discover that Nina Brun had gone there?"

"No, I cannot claim to have discovered that, or I should certainly have warned him at once when I found out—only recently—about the gang. As a matter of fact, the last information I had of Lord Seastoke was a line in yesterday's Morning Post to the effect that he was still at Cairo. But many of these pieces—" He brushed his finger almost lovingly across the vivid chariot race that embellished the reverse of the coin, and broke off to remark: "You really ought to take up the subject, Louis. You have no idea how useful it might prove to you some day."

"I really think I must," replied Carlyle grimly. "Two hundred and fifty pounds the original of this cost, I believe."

"Cheap, too; it would make five hundred pounds in New York to-day. As I was saying, many are literally unique. This gem by Kimon is—here is his signature, you see; Peter is particularly good at lettering—and as I handled the genuine tetradrachm about two years ago, when Lord Seastoke exhibited it at a meeting of our society in Albemarle Street, there is nothing at all wonderful in my being able to fix the locale of your mystery. Indeed, I feel that I ought to apologize for it all being so simple."

"I think," remarked Mr. Carlyle, critically examining the loose threads on his left boot, "that the apology on that head would be more appropriate from me."

THE KNIGHT'S CROSS SIGNAL PROBLEM

"Louis," exclaimed Mr. Carrados, with the air of genial gaiety that Carlyle had found so incongruous to his conception of a blind man, "you have a mystery somewhere about you! I know it by your step."

Nearly a month had passed since the incident of the false Dionysius had led to the two men meeting. It was now December. Whatever Mr. Carlyle's step might indicate to the inner eye it betokened to the casual observer the manner of a crisp, alert, self-possessed man of business. Carlyle, in truth, betrayed nothing of the pessimism and despondency that had marked him on the earlier occasion.

"You have only yourself to thank that it is a very poor one," he retorted. "If you hadn't held me to a hasty promise—"

"To give me an option on the next case that baffled you, no matter what it was—"

"Just so. The consequence is that you get a very unsatisfactory affair that has no special interest to an amateur and is only baffling because it is—well—"

"Well, baffling?"

"Exactly, Max. Your would-be jest has discovered the proverbial truth. I need hardly tell you that it is only the insoluble that is finally baffling and this is very probably insoluble. You remember the awful smash on the Central and Suburban at Knight's Cross Station a few weeks ago?"

"Yes," replied Carrados, with interest. "I read the whole ghastly details at the time."

"You read?" exclaimed his friend suspiciously.

"I still use the familiar phrases," explained Carrados, with a smile. "As a matter of fact, my secretary reads to me. I mark what I want to hear and when he comes at ten o'clock we clear off the morning papers in no time."

"And how do you know what to mark?" demanded Mr. Carlyle cunningly.

Carrados's right hand, lying idly on the table, moved to a newspaper near. He ran his finger along a column heading, his eyes still turned towards his visitor.

"'The Money Market. Continued from page 2. British Railways,'" he announced.

"Extraordinary," murmured Carlyle.

"Not very," said Carrados. "If someone dipped a stick in treacle and wrote 'Rats' across a marble slab you would probably be able to distinguish what was there, blindfold."

"Probably," admitted Mr. Carlyle. "At all events we will not test the experiment."

"The difference to you of treacle on a marble background is scarcely greater than that of printers' ink on newspaper to me. But anything smaller than pica I do not read with comfort, and below long primer I cannot read at all. Hence the secretary. Now the accident, Louis."

"The accident: well, you remember all about that. An ordinary Central and Suburban passenger train, non-stop at Knight's Cross, ran past the signal and crashed into a crowded electric train that was just beginning to move out. It was like sending a garden roller down a row of handlights. Two carriages of the electric train were flattened out of existence; the next two were broken up. For the first time on an English railway there was a good stand-up smash between a heavy steam-engine and a train of light cars, and it was 'bad for the coo.'"

"Twenty-seven killed, forty something injured, eight died since," commented Carrados.

"That was bad for the Co.," said Carlyle. "Well, the main fact was plain enough. The heavy train was in the wrong. But was the engine-driver responsible? He claimed, and he claimed vehemently from the first, and he never varied one iota, that he had a 'clear' signal—that is to say, the green light, it being dark. The signalman concerned was equally dogged that he never pulled off the signal—that it was at 'danger' when the accident happened and that it had been for five minutes before. Obviously, they could not both be right."

"Why, Louis?" asked Mr. Carrados smoothly.

"The signal must either have been up or down—red or green."

"Did you ever notice the signals on the Great Northern Railway, Louis?"

"Not particularly, Why?"

"One winterly day, about the year when you and I were concerned in being born, the engine-driver of a Scotch express received the 'clear' from a signal near a little Huntingdon station called Abbots Ripton. He went on and crashed into a goods train and into the thick of the smash a down express mowed its way. Thirteen killed and the usual tale of injured. He was positive that the signal gave him a 'clear'; the signalman was equally confident that he had never pulled it off the 'danger.' Both were right, and yet the signal was in working order. As I said, it was a winterly day; it had been snowing hard and the snow froze and accumulated on the upper edge of the signal arm until its weight bore it down. That is a fact that no fiction writer dare have invented, but to this day every signal on the Great Northern pivots from the centre of the arm instead of from the end, in memory of that snowstorm."

"That came out at the inquest, I presume?" said Mr. Carlyle. "We have had the Board of Trade inquiry and the inquest here and no explanation is forthcoming. Everything was in perfect order. It rests between the word of the signalman and the word of the engine-driver—not a jot of direct evidence either way. Which is right?"

"That is what you are going to find out, Louis?" suggested Carrados.

"It is what I am being paid for finding out," admitted Mr. Carlyle frankly. "But so far we are just where the inquest left it, and, between ourselves, I candidly can't see an inch in front of my face in the matter."

"Nor can I," said the blind man, with a rather wry smile. "Never mind. The engine-driver is your client, of course?"

"Yes," admitted Carlyle. "But how the deuce did you know?"

"Let us say that your sympathies are enlisted on his behalf. The jury were inclined to exonerate the signalman, weren't they? What has the company done with your man?"

"Both are suspended. Hutchins, the driver, hears that he may probably be given charge of a lavatory at one of the stations. He is a decent, bluff, short-spoken old chap, with his heart in his work. Just now you'll find him at his worst—bitter and suspicious. The thought of swabbing down a lavatory and taking pennies all day is poisoning him."

"Naturally. Well, there we have honest Hutchins: taciturn, a little touchy perhaps, grown grey in the service of the company, and manifesting quite a bulldog-like devotion to his favourite 538."

"Why, that actually was the number of his engine—how do you know it?" demanded Carlyle sharply.

"It was mentioned two or three times at the inquest, Louis," replied Carrados mildly.

"And you remembered—with no reason to?"

"You can generally trust a blind man's memory, especially if he has taken the trouble to develop it."

"Then you will remember that Hutchins did not make a very good impression at the time. He was surly and irritable under the ordeal. I want you to see the case from all sides."

"He called the signalman—Mead—a 'lying young dog,' across the room, I believe. Now, Mead, what is he like? You have seen him, of course?"

"Yes. He does not impress me favourably. He is glib, ingratiating, and distinctly 'greasy.' He has a ready answer for everything almost before the question is out of your mouth. He has thought of everything."

"And now you are going to tell me something, Louis," said Carrados encouragingly.

Mr. Carlyle laughed a little to cover an involuntary movement of surprise.

"There is a suggestive line that was not touched at the inquiries," he admitted. "Hutchins has been a saving man all his life, and he has received good wages. Among his class he is regarded as wealthy. I daresay that he has five hundred pounds in the bank. He is a widower with one daughter, a very nice-mannered girl of about twenty. Mead is a young man, and he and the girl are sweethearts—have been informally engaged for some time. But old Hutchins would not hear of it; he seems to have taken a dislike to the signalman from the first, and latterly he had forbidden him to come to his house or his daughter to speak to him."

"Excellent, Louis," cried Carrados in great delight. "We shall clear your man in a blaze of red and green lights yet and hang the glib, 'greasy' signalman from his own signal-post."

"It is a significant fact, seriously?"

"It is absolutely convincing."

"It may have been a slip, a mental lapse on Mead's part which he discovered the moment it was too late, and then, being too cowardly to admit his fault, and having so much at stake, he took care to make detection impossible. It may have been that, but my idea is rather that probably it was neither quite pure accident nor pure design. I can imagine Mead meanly pluming himself over the fact that the life of this man who stands in his way, and whom he must cordially dislike, lies in his power. I can imagine the idea becoming an obsession as he dwells on it. A dozen times with his hand on the lever he lets his mind explore the possibilities of a moment's defection. Then one day he pulls the signal off in sheer bravado—and hastily puts it at danger again. He may have done it once or he may have done it oftener before he was caught in a fatal moment of irresolution. The chances are about even that the engine-driver would be killed. In any case he would be disgraced, for it is easier on the face of it to believe that a man might run past a danger signal in absentmindedness, without noticing it, than that a man should pull off a signal and replace it without being conscious of his actions."

"The fireman was killed. Does your theory involve the certainty of the fireman being killed, Louis?"

"No," said Carlyle. "The fireman is a difficulty, but looking at it from Mead's point of view—whether he has been guilty of an error or a crime—it resolves itself into this: First, the fireman may be killed. Second, he may not notice the signal at all. Third, in any case he will loyally corroborate his driver and the good old jury will discount that."

Carrados smoked thoughtfully, his open, sightless eyes merely appearing to be set in a tranquil gaze across the room.

"It would not be an improbable explanation," he said presently. "Ninety-nine men out of a hundred would say: 'People do not do these things.' But you and I, who have in our different ways studied criminology, know that they sometimes do, or else there would be no curious crimes. What have you done on that line?"

To anyone who could see, Mr. Carlyle's expression conveyed an answer.

"You are behind the scenes, Max. What was there for me to do? Still I must do something for my money. Well, I have had a very close inquiry made confidentially among the men. There might be a whisper of one of them knowing more than had come out—a man restrained by friendship, or enmity, or even grade jealousy. Nothing came of that. Then there was the remote chance that some private person had noticed the signal without attaching any importance to it then, one who would be able to identify it still by something associated with the time. I went over the line myself. Opposite the signal the line on one side is shut in by a high blank wall; on the other side are houses, but coming below the butt-end of a scullery the signal does not happen to be visible from any road or from any window."

"My poor Louis!" said Carrados, in friendly ridicule. "You were at the end of your tether?"

"I was," admitted Carlyle. "And now that you know the sort of job it is I don't suppose that you are keen on wasting your time over it."

"That would hardly be fair, would it?" said Carrados reasonably. "No, Louis, I will take over your honest old driver and your greasy young signalman and your fatal signal that cannot be seen from anywhere."

"But it is an important point for you to remember, Max, that although the signal cannot be seen from the box, if the mechanism had gone wrong, or anyone tampered with the arm, the automatic indicator would at once have told Mead that the green light was showing. Oh, I have gone very thoroughly into the technical points, I assure you."

"I must do so too," commented Mr. Carrados gravely.

"For that matter, if there is anything you want to know, I dare say that I can tell you," suggested his visitor. "It might save your time."

"True," acquiesced Carrados. "I should like to know whether anyone belonging to the houses that bound the line there came of age or got married on the twenty-sixth of November."

Mr. Carlyle looked across curiously at his host.

"I really do not know, Max," he replied, in his crisp, precise way. "What on earth has that got to do with it, may I inquire?"

"The only explanation of the Pont St. Lin swing-bridge disaster of '75 was the reflection of a green bengal light on a cottage window."

Mr. Carlyle smiled his indulgence privately.

"My dear chap, you mustn't let your retentive memory of obscure happenings run away with you," he remarked wisely. "In nine cases out of ten the obvious explanation is the true one. The difficulty, as here, lies in proving it. Now, you would like to see these men?"

"I expect so; in any case, I will see Hutchins first."

"Both live in Holloway. Shall I ask Hutchins to come here to see you—say to-morrow? He is doing nothing."

"No," replied Carrados. "To-morrow I must call on my brokers and my time may be filled up."

"Quite right; you mustn't neglect your own affairs for this—experiment," assented Carlyle.

"Besides, I should prefer to drop in on Hutchins at his own home. Now, Louis, enough of the honest old man for one night. I have a lovely thing by Eumenes that I want to show you. To-day is—Tuesday. Come to dinner on Sunday and pour the vials of your ridicule on my want of success."

"That's an amiable way of putting it," replied Carlyle. "All right, I will."

Two hours later Carrados was again in his study, apparently, for a wonder, sitting idle. Sometimes he smiled to himself, and once or twice he laughed a little, but for the most part his pleasant, impassive face reflected no emotion and he sat with his useless eyes tranquilly fixed on an unseen distance. It was a fantastic caprice of the man to mock his sightlessness by a parade of light, and under the soft brilliance of a dozen electric brackets the room was as bright as day. At length he stood up and rang the bell.

"I suppose Mr. Greatorex isn't still here by any chance, Parkinson?" he asked, referring to his secretary.

"I think not, sir, but I will ascertain," replied the man.

"Never mind. Go to his room and bring me the last two files of The Times. Now"—when he returned—"turn to the earliest you have there. The date?"

"November the second."

"That will do. Find the Money Market; it will be in the Supplement. Now look down the columns until you come to British Railways."

"I have it, sir."

"Central and Suburban. Read the closing price and the change."

"Central and Suburban Ordinary, 66-1/2-67-1/2, fall 1/8. Preferred Ordinary, 81-81-1/2, no change. Deferred Ordinary, 27-1/2-27-3/4, fall 1/4. That is all, sir."

"Now take a paper about a week on. Read the Deferred only."

"27-27-1/4, no change."

"Another week."

"29-1/2-30, rise 5/8."

"Another."

"31-1/2-32-1/2, rise 1."

"Very good. Now on Tuesday the twenty-seventh November."

"31-7/8-32-3/4, rise 1/2."

"Yes. The next day."

"24-1/2-23-1/2, fall 9."

"Quite so, Parkinson. There had been an accident, you see."

"Yes, sir. Very unpleasant accident. Jane knows a person whose sister's young man has a cousin who had his arm torn off in it—torn off at the socket, she says, sir. It seems to bring it home to one, sir."

"That is all. Stay—in the paper you have, look down the first money column and see if there is any reference to the Central and Suburban."

"Yes, sir. 'City and Suburbans, which after their late depression on the projected extension of the motor bus service, had been steadily creeping up on the abandonment of the scheme, and as a result of their own excellent traffic returns, suffered a heavy slump through the lamentable accident of Thursday night. The Deferred in particular at one time fell eleven points as it was felt that the possible dividend, with which rumour has of late been busy, was now out of the question.'"

"Yes; that is all. Now you can take the papers back. And let it be a warning to you, Parkinson, not to invest your savings in speculative railway deferreds."

"Yes, sir. Thank you, sir, I will endeavour to remember." He lingered for a moment as he shook the file of papers level. "I may say, sir, that I have my eye on a small block of cottage property at Acton. But even cottage property scarcely seems safe from legislative depredation now, sir."

The next day Mr. Carrados called on his brokers in the city. It is to be presumed that he got through his private business quicker than he expected, for after leaving Austin Friars he continued his journey to

Holloway, where he found Hutchins at home and sitting morosely before his kitchen fire. Rightly assuming that his luxuriant car would involve him in a certain amount of public attention in Klondyke Street, the blind man dismissed it some distance from the house, and walked the rest of the way, guided by the almost imperceptible touch of Parkinson's arm.

"Here is a gentleman to see you, father," explained Miss Hutchins, who had come to the door. She divined the relative positions of the two visitors at a glance.

"Then why don't you take him into the parlour?" grumbled the ex-driver. His face was a testimonial of hard work and general sobriety but at the moment one might hazard from his voice and manner that he had been drinking earlier in the day.

"I don't think that the gentleman would be impressed by the difference between our parlour and our kitchen," replied the girl quaintly, "and it is warmer here."

"What's the matter with the parlour now?" demanded her father sourly. "It was good enough for your mother and me. It used to be good enough for you."

"There is nothing the matter with it, nor with the kitchen either." She turned impassively to the two who had followed her along the narrow passage. "Will you go in, sir?"

"I don't want to see no gentleman," cried Hutchins noisily. "Unless"—his manner suddenly changed to one of pitiable anxiety—"unless you're from the Company sir, to—to—"

"No; I have come on Mr. Carlyle's behalf," replied Carrados, walking to a chair as though he moved by a kind of instinct.

Hutchins laughed his wry contempt.

"Mr. Carlyle!" he reiterated; "Mr. Carlyle! Fat lot of good he's been. Why don't he do something for his money?"

"He has," replied Carrados, with imperturbable good-humour; "he has sent me. Now, I want to ask you a few questions."

"A few questions!" roared the irate man. "Why, blast it, I have done nothing else but answer questions for a month. I didn't pay Mr. Carlyle to ask me questions; I can get enough of that for nixes. Why don't you go and ask Mr. Herbert Ananias Mead your few questions—then you might find out something."

There was a slight movement by the door and Carrados knew that the girl had quietly left the room.

"You saw that, sir?" demanded the father, diverted to a new line of bitterness. "You saw that girl—my own daughter, that I've worked for all her life?"

"No," replied Carrados.

"The girl that's just gone out—she's my daughter," explained Hutchins.

"I know, but I did not see her. I see nothing. I am blind."

"Blind!" exclaimed the old fellow, sitting up in startled wonderment. "You mean it, sir? You walk all right and you look at me as if you saw me. You're kidding surely."

"No," smiled Carrados. "It's quite right."

"Then it's a funny business, sir—you what are blind expecting to find something that those with their eyes couldn't," ruminated Hutchins sagely.

"There are things that you can't see with your eyes, Hutchins."

"Perhaps you are right, sir. Well, what is it you want to know?"

"Light a cigar first," said the blind man, holding out his case and waiting until the various sounds told him that his host was smoking contentedly. "The train you were driving at the time of the accident was the six-twenty-seven from Notcliff. It stopped everywhere until it reached Lambeth Bridge, the chief London station on your line. There it became something of an express, and leaving Lambeth Bridge at seven-eleven, should not stop again until it fetched Swanstead on Thames, eleven miles out, at seven-thirty-four. Then it stopped on and off from Swanstead to Ingerfield, the terminus of that branch, which it reached at eight-five."

Hutchins nodded, and then, remembering, said: "That's right, sir."

"That was your business all day—running between Notcliff and Ingerfield?"

"Yes, sir. Three journeys up and three down mostly."

"With the same stops on all the down journeys?"

"No. The seven-eleven is the only one that does a run from the Bridge to Swanstead. You see, it is just on the close of the evening rush, as they call it. A good many late business gentlemen living at Swanstead use the seven-eleven regular. The other journeys we stop at every station to Lambeth Bridge, and then here and there beyond."

"There are, of course, other trains doing exactly the same journey—a service, in fact?"

"Yes, sir. About six."

"And do any of those—say, during the rush—do any of those run non-stop from Lambeth to Swanstead?"

Hutchins reflected a moment. All the choler and restlessness had melted out of the man's face. He was again the excellent artisan, slow but capable and self-reliant.

"That I couldn't definitely say, sir. Very few short-distance trains pass the junction, but some of those may. A guide would show us in a minute but I haven't got one."

"Never mind. You said at the inquest that it was no uncommon thing for you to be pulled up at the 'stop' signal east of Knight's Cross Station. How often would that happen—only with the seven-eleven, mind."

"Perhaps three times a week; perhaps twice."

"The accident was on a Thursday. Have you noticed that you were pulled up oftener on a Thursday than on any other day?"

A smile crossed the driver's face at the question.

"You don't happen to live at Swanstead yourself, sir?" he asked in reply.

"No," admitted Carrados. "Why?"

"Well, sir, we were always pulled up on Thursday; practically always, you may say. It got to be quite a saying among those who used the train regular; they used to look out for it."

Carrados's sightless eyes had the one quality of concealing emotion supremely. "Oh," he commented softly, "always; and it was quite a saying, was it? And why was it always so on Thursday?"

"It had to do with the early closing, I'm told. The suburban traffic was a bit different. By rights we ought to have been set back two minutes for that day, but I suppose it wasn't thought worth while to alter us in the time-table so we most always had to wait outside Three Deep tunnel for a west-bound electric to make good."

"You were prepared for it then?"

"Yes, sir, I was," said Hutchins, reddening at some recollection, "and very down about it was one of the jury over that. But, mayhap once in three months, I did get through even on a Thursday, and it's not for me to question whether things are right or wrong just because they are not what I may expect. The signals are my orders, sir—stop! go on! and it's for me to obey, as you would a general on the field of battle. What would happen otherwise! It was nonsense what they said about going cautious; and the man who stated it was a barber who didn't know the difference between a 'distance' and a 'stop' signal down to the minute they gave their verdict. My orders, sir, given me by that signal, was 'Go right ahead and keep to your running time!'"

Carrados nodded a soothing assent. "That is all, I think," he remarked.

"All!" exclaimed Hutchins in surprise. "Why, sir, you can't have got much idea of it yet."

"Quite enough. And I know it isn't pleasant for you to be taken along the same ground over and over again."

The man moved awkwardly in his chair and pulled nervously at his grizzled beard.

"You mustn't take any notice of what I said just now, sir," he apologized. "You somehow make me feel that something may come of it; but I've been badgered about and accused and cross-examined from one to another of them these weeks till it's fairly made me bitter against everything. And now they talk of putting me in a lavatory—me that has been with the company for five and forty years and on the foot-plate thirty-two—a man suspected of running past a danger signal."

"You have had a rough time, Hutchins; you will have to exercise your patience a little longer yet," said Carrados sympathetically.

"You think something may come of it, sir? You think you will be able to clear me? Believe me, sir, if you could give me something to look forward to it might save me from—" He pulled himself up and shook his head sorrowfully. "I've been near it," he added simply.

Carrados reflected and took his resolution.

"To-day is Wednesday. I think you may hope to hear something from your general manager towards the middle of next week."

"Good God, sir! You really mean that?"

"In the interval show your good sense by behaving reasonably. Keep civilly to yourself and don't talk. Above all"—he nodded towards a quart jug that stood on the table between them, an incident that filled the simple-minded engineer with boundless wonder when he recalled it afterwards—"above all, leave that alone."

Hutchins snatched up the vessel and brought it crashing down on the hearthstone, his face shining with a set resolution.

"I've done with it, sir. It was the bitterness and despair that drove me to that. Now I can do without it."

The door was hastily opened and Miss Hutchins looked anxiously from her father to the visitors and back again.

"Oh, whatever is the matter?" she exclaimed. "I heard a great crash."

"This gentleman is going to clear me, Meg, my dear," blurted out the old man irrepressibly. "And I've done with the drink for ever."

"Hutchins! Hutchins!" said Carrados warningly.

"My daughter, sir; you wouldn't have her not know?" pleaded Hutchins, rather crest-fallen. "It won't go any further."

Carrados laughed quietly to himself as he felt Margaret Hutchins's startled and questioning eyes attempting to read his mind. He shook hands with the engine-driver without further comment, however, and walked out into the commonplace little street under Parkinson's unobtrusive guidance.

"Very nice of Miss Hutchins to go into half-mourning, Parkinson," he remarked as they went along. "Thoughtful, and yet not ostentatious."

"Yes, sir," agreed Parkinson, who had long ceased to wonder at his master's perceptions.

"The Romans, Parkinson, had a saying to the effect that gold carries no smell. That is a pity sometimes. What jewellery did Miss Hutchins wear?"

"Very little, sir. A plain gold brooch representing a merry-thought—the merry-thought of a sparrow, I should say, sir. The only other article was a smooth-backed gun-metal watch, suspended from a gun-metal bow."

"Nothing showy or expensive, eh?"

"Oh dear no, sir. Quite appropriate for a young person of her position."

"Just what I should have expected." He slackened his pace. "We are passing a hoarding, are we not?"

"Yes, sir."

"We will stand here a moment. Read me the letterpress of the poster before us."

"This 'Oxo' one, sir?"

"Yes."

"'Oxo,' sir."

Carrados was convulsed with silent laughter. Parkinson had infinitely more dignity and conceded merely a tolerant recognition of the ludicrous.

"That was a bad shot, Parkinson," remarked his master when he could speak. "We will try another."

For three minutes, with scrupulous conscientiousness on the part of the reader and every appearance of keen interest on the part of the hearer, there were set forth the particulars of a sale by auction of superfluous timber and builders' material.

"That will do," said Carrados, when the last detail had been reached. "We can be seen from the door of No. 107 still?"

"Yes, sir."

"No indication of anyone coming to us from there?"

"No, sir."

Carrados walked thoughtfully on again. In the Holloway Road they rejoined the waiting motor-car.

"Lambeth Bridge Station" was the order the driver received.

From the station the car was sent on home and Parkinson was instructed to take two first-class singles for Richmond, which could be reached by changing at Stafford Road. The "evening rush" had not yet commenced and they had no difficulty in finding an empty carriage when the train came in.

Parkinson was kept busy that journey describing what he saw at various points between Lambeth Bridge and Knight's Cross. For a quarter of a mile Carrados's demands on the eyes and the memory of his remarkable servant were wide and incessant. Then his questions ceased. They had passed the "stop" signal, east of Knight's Cross Station.

The following afternoon they made the return journey as far as Knight's Cross. This time, however, the surroundings failed to interest Carrados. "We are going to look at some rooms," was the information he offered on the subject, and an imperturbable "Yes, sir" had been the extent of Parkinson's comment on the unusual proceeding. After leaving the station they turned sharply along a road that ran parallel with the line, a dull thoroughfare of substantial, elderly houses that were beginning to sink into decrepitude. Here and there a corner residence displayed the brass plate of a professional occupant, but for the most part they were given up to the various branches of second-rate apartment letting.

"The third house after the one with the flagstaff," said Carrados.

Parkinson rang the bell, which was answered by a young servant, who took an early opportunity of assuring them that she was not tidy as it was rather early in the afternoon. She informed Carrados, in reply to his inquiry, that Miss Chubb was at home, and showed them into a melancholy little sitting-room to await her appearance.

"I shall be 'almost' blind here, Parkinson," remarked Carrados, walking about the room. "It saves explanation."

"Very good, sir," replied Parkinson.

Five minutes later, an interval suggesting that Miss Chubb also found it rather early in the afternoon, Carrados was arranging to take rooms for his attendant and himself for the short time that he would be in London, seeing an oculist.

"One bedroom, mine, must face north," he stipulated. "It has to do with the light."

Miss Chubb replied that she quite understood. Some gentlemen, she added, had their requirements, others their fancies. She endeavoured to suit all. The bedroom she had in view from the first did face north. She would not have known, only the last gentleman, curiously enough, had made the same request.

"A sufferer like myself?" inquired Carrados affably.

Miss Chubb did not think so. In his case she regarded it merely as a fancy. He had said that he could not sleep on any other side. She had had to turn out of her own room to accommodate him, but if one kept an apartment-house one had to be adaptable; and Mr. Ghoosh was certainly very liberal in his ideas.

"Ghoosh? An Indian gentleman, I presume?" hazarded Carrados.

It appeared that Mr. Ghoosh was an Indian. Miss Chubb confided that at first she had been rather perturbed at the idea of taking in "a black man," as she confessed to regarding him. She reiterated, however, that Mr. Ghoosh proved to be "quite the gentleman." Five minutes of affability put Carrados in full possession of Mr. Ghoosh's manner of life and movements—the dates of his arrival and departure, his solitariness and his daily habits.

"This would be the best bedroom," said Miss Chubb.

It was a fair-sized room on the first floor. The window looked out on to the roof of an outbuilding; beyond, the deep cutting of the railway line. Opposite stood the dead wall that Mr. Carlyle had spoken of.

Carrados "looked" round the room with the discriminating glance that sometimes proved so embarrassing to those who knew him.

"I have to take a little daily exercise," he remarked, walking to the window and running his hand up the woodwork. "You will not mind my fixing a 'developer' here, Miss Chubb—a few small screws?"

Miss Chubb thought not. Then she was sure not. Finally she ridiculed the idea of minding with scorn.

"If there is width enough," mused Carrados, spanning the upright critically. "Do you happen to have a wooden foot-rule convenient?"

"Well, to be sure!" exclaimed Miss Chubb, opening a rapid succession of drawers until she produced the required article. "When we did out this room after Mr. Ghoosh, there was this very ruler among the things that he hadn't thought worth taking. This is what you require, sir?"

"Yes," replied Carrados, accepting it, "I think this is exactly what I require." It was a common new white-wood rule, such as one might buy at any small stationer's for a penny. He carelessly took off the width of the upright, reading the figures with a touch; and then continued to run a finger-tip delicately up and down the edges of the instrument.

"Four and seven-eighths," was his unspoken conclusion.

"I hope it will do sir."

"Admirably," replied Carrados. "But I haven't reached the end of my requirements yet, Miss Chubb."

"No, sir?" said the landlady, feeling that it would be a pleasure to oblige so agreeable a gentleman, "what else might there be?"

"Although I can see very little I like to have a light, but not any kind of light. Gas I cannot do with. Do you think that you would be able to find me an oil lamp?"

"Certainly, sir. I got out a very nice brass lamp that I have specially for Mr. Ghoosh. He read a good deal of an evening and he preferred a lamp."

"That is very convenient. I suppose it is large enough to burn for a whole evening?"

"Yes, indeed. And very particular he was always to have it filled every day."

"A lamp without oil is not very useful," smiled Carrados, following her towards another room, and absent-mindedly slipping the foot-rule into his pocket.

Whatever Parkinson thought of the arrangement of going into second-rate apartments in an obscure street it is to be inferred that his devotion to his master was sufficient to overcome his private emotions as a self-respecting "man." At all events, as they were approaching the station he asked, and without a trace of feeling, whether there were any orders for him with reference to the proposed migration.

"None, Parkinson," replied his master. "We must be satisfied with our present quarters."

"I beg your pardon, sir," said Parkinson, with some constraint. "I understand that you had taken the rooms for a week certain."

"I am afraid that Miss Chubb will be under the same impression. Unforeseen circumstances will prevent our going, however. Mr. Greatorex must write to-morrow, enclosing a cheque, with my regrets, and adding a penny for this ruler which I seem to have brought away with me. It, at least, is something for the money."

Parkinson may be excused for not attempting to understand the course of events.

"Here is your train coming in, sir," he merely said.

"We will let it go and wait for another. Is there a signal at either end of the platform?"

"Yes, sir; at the further end."

"Let us walk towards it. Are there any of the porters or officials about here?"

"No, sir; none."

"Take this ruler. I want you to go up the steps—there are steps up the signal, by the way?"

"Yes, sir."

"I want you to measure the glass of the lamp. Do not go up any higher than is necessary, but if you have to stretch be careful not to mark off the measurement with your nail, although the impulse is a natural one. That has been done already."

Parkinson looked apprehensively round and about. Fortunately the part was a dark and unfrequented spot and everyone else was moving towards the exit at the other end of the platform. Fortunately, also, the signal was not a high one.

"As near as I can judge on the rounded surface, the glass is four and seven-eighths across," reported Parkinson.

"Thank you," replied Carrados, returning the measure to his pocket, "four and seven-eighths is quite near enough. Now we will take the next train back."

Sunday evening came, and with it Mr. Carlyle to The Turrets at the appointed hour. He brought to the situation a mind poised for any eventuality and a trenchant eye. As the time went on and the impenetrable Carrados made no allusion to the case, Carlyle's manner inclined to a waggish commiseration of his host's position. Actually, he said little, but the crisp precision of his voice when the path lay open to a remark of any significance left little to be said.

It was not until they had finished dinner and returned to the library that Carrados gave the slightest hint of anything unusual being in the air. His first indication of coming events was to remove the key from the outside to the inside of the door.

"What are you doing, Max?" demanded Mr. Carlyle, his curiosity overcoming the indirect attitude.

"You have been very entertaining, Louis," replied his friend, "but Parkinson should be back very soon now and it is as well to be prepared. Do you happen to carry a revolver?"

"Not when I come to dine with you, Max," replied Carlyle, with all the aplomb he could muster. "Is it usual?"

Carrados smiled affectionately at his guest's agile recovery and touched the secret spring of a drawer in an antique bureau by his side. The little hidden receptacle shot smoothly out, disclosing a pair of dull-blued pistols.

"To-night, at all events, it might be prudent," he replied, handing one to Carlyle and putting the other into his own pocket. "Our man may be here at any minute, and we do not know in what temper he will come."

"Our man!" exclaimed Carlyle, craning forward in excitement. "Max! you don't mean to say that you have got Mead to admit it?"

"No one has admitted it," said Carrados. "And it is not Mead."

"Not Mead.... Do you mean that Hutchins—?"

"Neither Mead nor Hutchins. The man who tampered with the signal—for Hutchins was right and a green light was exhibited—is a young Indian from Bengal. His name is Drishna and he lives at Swanstead."

Mr. Carlyle stared at his friend between sheer surprise and blank incredulity.

"You really mean this, Carrados?" he said.

"My fatal reputation for humour!" smiled Carrados. "If I am wrong, Louis, the next hour will expose it."

"But why—why—why? The colossal villainy, the unparalleled audacity!" Mr. Carlyle lost himself among incredulous superlatives and could only stare.

"Chiefly to get himself out of a disastrous speculation," replied Carrados, answering the question. "If there was another motive—or at least an incentive—which I suspect, doubtless we shall hear of it."

"All the same, Max, I don't think that you have treated me quite fairly," protested Carlyle, getting over his first surprise and passing to a sense of injury. "Here we are and I know nothing, absolutely nothing, of the whole affair."

"We both have our ideas of pleasantry, Louis," replied Carrados genially. "But I dare say you are right and perhaps there is still time to atone." In the fewest possible words he outlined the course of his investigations. "And now you know all that is to be known until Drishna arrives."

"But will he come?" questioned Carlyle doubtfully. "He may be suspicious."

"Yes, he will be suspicious."

"Then he will not come."

"On the contrary, Louis, he will come because my letter will make him suspicious. He is coming; otherwise Parkinson would have telephoned me at once and we should have had to take other measures."

"What did you say, Max?" asked Carlyle curiously.

"I wrote that I was anxious to discuss an Indo-Scythian inscription with him, and sent my car in the hope that he would be able to oblige me."

"But is he interested in Indo-Scythian inscriptions?"

"I haven't the faintest idea," admitted Carrados, and Mr. Carlyle was throwing up his hands in despair when the sound of a motor-car wheels softly kissing the gravel surface of the drive outside brought him to his feet.

"By Gad, you are right, Max!" he exclaimed, peeping through the curtains. "There is a man inside."

"Mr. Drishna," announced Parkinson a minute later.

The visitor came into the room with leisurely self-possession that might have been real or a desperate assumption. He was a slightly built young man of about twenty-five, with black hair and eyes, a small, carefully trained moustache, and a dark olive skin. His physiognomy was not displeasing, but his expression had a harsh and supercilious tinge. In attire he erred towards the immaculately spruce.

"Mr. Carrados?" he said inquiringly.

Carrados, who had risen, bowed slightly without offering his hand.

"This gentleman," he said, indicating his friend, "is Mr. Carlyle, the celebrated private detective."

The Indian shot a very sharp glance at the object of this description. Then he sat down.

"You wrote me a letter, Mr. Carrados," he remarked, in English that scarcely betrayed any foreign origin, "a rather curious letter, I may say. You asked me about an ancient inscription. I know nothing of antiquities; but I thought, as you had sent, that it would be more courteous if I came and explained this to you."

"That was the object of my letter," replied Carrados.

"You wished to see me?" said Drishna, unable to stand the ordeal of the silence that Carrados imposed after his remark.

"When you left Miss Chubb's house you left a ruler behind." One lay on the desk by Carrados and he took it up as he spoke.

"I don't understand what you are talking about," said Drishna guardedly. "You are making some mistake."

"The ruler was marked at four and seven-eighths inches—the measure of the glass of the signal lamp outside."

The unfortunate young man was unable to repress a start. His face lost its healthy tone. Then, with a sudden impulse, he made a step forward and snatched the object from Carrados's hand.

"If it is mine I have a right to it," he exclaimed, snapping the ruler in two and throwing it on to the back of the blazing fire. "It is nothing."

"Pardon me, I did not say that the one you have so impetuously disposed of was yours. As a matter of fact, it was mine. Yours is—elsewhere."

"Wherever it is you have no right to it if it is mine," panted Drishna, with rising excitement. "You are a thief, Mr. Carrados. I will not stay any longer here."

He jumped up and turned towards the door. Carlyle made a step forward, but the precaution was unnecessary.

"One moment, Mr. Drishna," interposed Carrados, in his smoothest tones. "It is a pity, after you have come so far, to leave without hearing of my investigations in the neighbourhood of Shaftesbury Avenue."

Drishna sat down again.

"As you like," he muttered. "It does not interest me."

"I wanted to obtain a lamp of a certain pattern," continued Carrados. "It seemed to me that the simplest explanation would be to say that I wanted it for a motor-car. Naturally I went to Long Acre. At the first shop I said: 'Wasn't it here that a friend of mine, an Indian gentleman, recently had a lamp made with a green glass that was nearly five inches across?' No, it was not there but they could make me one. At the next shop the same; at the third, and fourth, and so on. Finally my persistence was rewarded. I found the place where the lamp had been made, and at the cost of ordering another I obtained all the details I wanted. It was news to them, the shopman informed me, that in some parts of India green was the danger colour and therefore tail lamps had to show a green light. The incident made some impression on him and he would be able to identify their customer—who paid in advance and gave no address—among a thousand of his countrymen. Do I succeed in interesting you, Mr. Drishna?"

"Do you?" replied Drishna, with a languid yawn. "Do I look interested?"

"You must make allowance for my unfortunate blindness," apologized Carrados, with grim irony.

"Blindness!" exclaimed Drishna, dropping his affectation of unconcern as though electrified by the word, "do you mean—really blind—that you do not see me?"

"Alas, no," admitted Carrados.

The Indian withdrew his right hand from his coat pocket and with a tragic gesture flung a heavy revolver down on the table between them.

"I have had you covered all the time, Mr. Carrados, and if I had wished to go and you or your friend had raised a hand to stop me, it would have been at the peril of your lives," he said, in a voice of melancholy triumph. "But what is the use of defying fate, and who successfully evades his destiny? A month ago I went to see one of our people who reads the future and sought to know the course of certain events. 'You need fear no human eye,' was the message given to me. Then she added: 'But when the sightless sees the unseen, make your peace with Yama.' And I thought she spoke of the Great Hereafter!"

"This amounts to an admission of your guilt," exclaimed Mr. Carlyle practically.

"I bow to the decree of fate," replied Drishna. "And it is fitting to the universal irony of existence that a blind man should be the instrument. I don't imagine, Mr. Carlyle," he added maliciously, "that you, with your eyes, would ever have brought that result about."

"You are a very cold-blooded young scoundrel, sir!" retorted Mr. Carlyle. "Good heavens! do you realize that you are responsible for the death of scores of innocent men and women?"

"Do you realize, Mr. Carlyle, that you and your Government and your soldiers are responsible for the death of thousands of innocent men and women in my country every day? If England was occupied by the Germans who quartered an army and an administration with their wives and their families and all their expensive paraphernalia on the unfortunate country until the whole nation was reduced to the verge of famine, and the appointment of every new official meant the callous death sentence on a thousand men and women to pay his salary, then if you went to Berlin and wrecked a train you would be hailed a patriot. What Boadicea did and—and Samson, so have I. If they were heroes, so am I."

"Well, upon my word!" cried the highly scandalized Carlyle, "what next! Boadicea was a—er—semi-legendary person, whom we may possibly admire at a distance. Personally, I do not profess to express an opinion. But Samson, I would remind you, is a Biblical character. Samson was mocked as an enemy. You, I do not doubt, have been entertained as a friend."

"And haven't I been mocked and despised and sneered at every day of my life here by your supercilious, superior, empty-headed men?" flashed back Drishna, his eyes leaping into malignity and his voice trembling with sudden passion. "Oh! how I hated them as I passed them in the street and recognized by a thousand petty insults their lordly English contempt for me as an inferior being—a nigger. How I longed with Caligula that a nation had a single neck that I might destroy it at one blow. I loathe you in your complacent hypocrisy, Mr. Carlyle, despise and utterly abominate you from an eminence of superiority that you can never even understand."

"I think we are getting rather away from the point, Mr. Drishna," interposed Carrados, with the impartiality of a judge. "Unless I am misinformed, you are not so ungallant as to include everyone you have met here in your execration?"

"Ah, no," admitted Drishna, descending into a quite ingenuous frankness. "Much as I hate your men I love your women. How is it possible that a nation should be so divided—its men so dull-witted and offensive, its women so quick, sympathetic and capable of appreciating?"

"But a little expensive, too, at times?" suggested Carrados.

Drishna sighed heavily.

"Yes; it is incredible. It is the generosity of their large nature. My allowance, though what most of you would call noble, has proved quite inadequate. I was compelled to borrow money and the interest became overwhelming. Bankruptcy was impracticable because I should have then been recalled by my people, and much as I detest England a certain reason made the thought of leaving it unbearable."

"Connected with the Arcady Theatre?"

"You know? Well, do not let us introduce the lady's name. In order to restore myself I speculated on the Stock Exchange. My credit was good through my father's position and the standing of the firm to which I am attached. I heard on reliable authority, and very early, that the Central and Suburban, and the Deferred especially, was safe to fall heavily, through a motor bus amalgamation that was then a secret. I opened a bear account and sold largely. The shares fell, but only fractionally, and I waited. Then, unfortunately, they began to go up. Adverse forces were at work and rumours were put about. I could not stand the settlement, and in order to carry over an account I was literally compelled to deal temporarily with some securities that were not technically my own property."

"Embezzlement, sir," commented Mr. Carlyle icily. "But what is embezzlement on the top of wholesale murder!"

"That is what it is called. In my case, however, it was only to be temporary. Unfortunately, the rise continued. Then, at the height of my despair, I chanced to be returning to Swanstead rather earlier than usual one evening, and the train was stopped at a certain signal to let another pass. There was conversation in the carriage and I learned certain details. One said that there would be an accident some day, and so forth. In a flash—as by an inspiration—I saw how the circumstance might be turned to account. A bad accident and the shares would certainly fall and my position would be retrieved. I think Mr. Carrados has somehow learned the rest."

"Max," said Mr. Carlyle, with emotion, "is there any reason why you should not send your man for a police officer and have this monster arrested on his own confession without further delay?"

"Pray do so, Mr. Carrados," acquiesced Drishna. "I shall certainly be hanged, but the speech I shall prepare will ring from one end of India to the other; my memory will be venerated as that of a martyr; and the emancipation of my motherland will be hastened by my sacrifice."

"In other words," commented Carrados, "there will be disturbances at half-a-dozen disaffected places, a few unfortunate police will be clubbed to death, and possibly worse things may happen. That does not suit us, Mr. Drishna."

"And how do you propose to prevent it?" asked Drishna, with cool assurance.

"It is very unpleasant being hanged on a dark winter morning; very cold, very friendless, very inhuman. The long trial, the solitude and the confinement, the thoughts of the long sleepless night before, the hangman and the pinioning and the noosing of the rope, are apt to prey on the imagination. Only a very stupid man can take hanging easily."

"What do you want me to do instead, Mr. Carrados?" asked Drishna shrewdly.

Carrados's hand closed on the weapon that still lay on the table between them. Without a word he pushed it across.

"I see," commented Drishna, with a short laugh and a gleaming eye. "Shoot myself and hush it up to suit your purpose. Withhold my message to save the exposures of a trial, and keep the flame from the torch of insurrectionary freedom."

"Also," interposed Carrados mildly, "to save your worthy people a good deal of shame, and to save the lady who is nameless the unpleasant necessity of relinquishing the house and the income which you have just settled on her. She certainly would not then venerate your memory."

"What is that?"

"The transaction which you carried through was based on a felony and could not be upheld. The firm you dealt with will go to the courts, and the money, being directly traceable, will be held forfeit as no good consideration passed."

"Max!" cried Mr. Carlyle hotly, "you are not going to let this scoundrel cheat the gallows after all?"

"The best use you can make of the gallows is to cheat it, Louis," replied Carrados. "Have you ever reflected what human beings will think of us a hundred years hence?"

"Oh, of course I'm not really in favour of hanging," admitted Mr. Carlyle.

"Nobody really is. But we go on hanging. Mr. Drishna is a dangerous animal who for the sake of pacific animals must cease to exist. Let his barbarous exploit pass into oblivion with him. The disadvantages of spreading it broadcast immeasurably outweigh the benefits."

"I have considered," announced Drishna. "I will do as you wish."

"Very well," said Carrados. "Here is some plain notepaper. You had better write a letter to someone saying that the financial difficulties in which you are involved make life unbearable."

"But there are no financial difficulties—now."

"That does not matter in the least. It will be put down to an hallucination and taken as showing the state of your mind."

"But what guarantee have we that he will not escape?" whispered Mr. Carlyle.

"He cannot escape," replied Carrados tranquilly. "His identity is too clear."

"I have no intention of trying to escape," put in Drishna, as he wrote. "You hardly imagine that I have not considered this eventuality, do you?"

"All the same," murmured the ex-lawyer, "I should like to have a jury behind me. It is one thing to execute a man morally; it is another to do it almost literally."

"Is that all right?" asked Drishna, passing across the letter he had written.

Carrados smiled at this tribute to his perception.

"Quite excellent," he replied courteously. "There is a train at nine-forty. Will that suit you?"

Drishna nodded and stood up. Mr. Carlyle had a very uneasy feeling that he ought to do something but could not suggest to himself what.

The next moment he heard his friend heartily thanking the visitor for the assistance he had been in the matter of the Indo-Scythian inscription, as they walked across the hall together. Then a door closed.

"I believe that there is something positively uncanny about Max at times," murmured the perturbed gentleman to himself.

THE TRAGEDY AT BROOKBEND COTTAGE

"Max," said Mr. Carlyle, when Parkinson had closed the door behind him, "this is Lieutenant Hollyer, whom you consented to see."

"To hear," corrected Carrados, smiling straight into the healthy and rather embarrassed face of the stranger before him. "Mr. Hollyer knows of my disability?"

"Mr. Carlyle told me," said the young man, "but, as a matter of fact, I had heard of you before, Mr. Carrados, from one of our men. It was in connection with the foundering of the Ivan Saratov."

Carrados wagged his head in good-humoured resignation.

"And the owners were sworn to inviolable secrecy!" he exclaimed. "Well, it is inevitable, I suppose. Not another scuttling case, Mr. Hollyer?"

"No, mine is quite a private matter," replied the lieutenant. "My sister, Mrs. Creake—but Mr. Carlyle would tell you better than I can. He knows all about it."

"No, no; Carlyle is a professional. Let me have it in the rough, Mr. Hollyer. My ears are my eyes, you know."

"Very well, sir. I can tell you what there is to tell, right enough, but I feel that when all's said and done it must sound very little to another, although it seems important to me."

"We have occasionally found trifles of significance ourselves," said Carrados encouragingly. "Don't let that deter you."

This was the essence of Lieutenant Hollyer's narrative:

"I have a sister, Millicent, who is married to a man called Creake. She is about twenty-eight now and he is at least fifteen years older. Neither my mother (who has since died) nor I cared very much about Creake. We had nothing particular against him, except, perhaps, the moderate disparity of age, but none of us appeared to have anything in common. He was a dark, taciturn man, and his moody silence froze up conversation. As a result, of course, we didn't see much of each other."

"This, you must understand, was four or five years ago, Max," interposed Mr. Carlyle officiously.

Carrados maintained an uncompromising silence. Mr. Carlyle blew his nose and contrived to impart a hurt significance into the operation. Then Lieutenant Hollyer continued:

"Millicent married Creake after a very short engagement. It was a frightfully subdued wedding—more like a funeral to me. The man professed to have no relations and apparently he had scarcely any friends or business acquaintances. He was an agent for something or other and had an office off Holborn. I suppose he made a living out of it then, although we knew practically nothing of his private affairs, but I gather that it has been going down since, and I suspect that for the past few years they have been getting along almost entirely on Millicent's little income. You would like the particulars of that?"

"Please," assented Carrados.

"When our father died about seven years ago, he left three thousand pounds. It was invested in Canadian stock and brought in a little over a hundred a year. By his will my mother was to have the income of that for life and on her death it was to pass to Millicent, subject to the payment of a lump sum of five hundred pounds to me. But my father privately suggested to me that if I should have no particular use for the money at the time, he would propose my letting Millicent have the income of it until I did want it, as she would not be particularly well off. You see, Mr. Carrados, a great deal more had been spent on my education and advancement than on her; I had my pay, and, of course, I could look out for myself better than a girl could."

"Quite so," agreed Carrados.

"Therefore I did nothing about that," continued the lieutenant. "Three years ago I was over again but I did not see much of them. They were living in lodgings. That was the only time since the marriage that I have seen them until last week. In the meanwhile our mother had died and Millicent had been receiving her income. She wrote me several letters at the time. Otherwise we did not correspond much, but about a year ago she sent me their new address—Brookbend Cottage, Mulling Common—a house that they had taken. When I got two months' leave I invited myself there as a matter of course, fully expecting to stay most of my time with them, but I made an excuse to get away after a week. The place was dismal and unendurable, the whole life and atmosphere indescribably depressing." He looked round with an instinct of caution, leaned forward earnestly, and dropped his voice. "Mr. Carrados, it is my absolute conviction that Creake is only waiting for a favourable opportunity to murder Millicent."

"Go on," said Carrados quietly. "A week of the depressing surroundings of Brookbend Cottage would not alone convince you of that, Mr. Hollyer."

"I am not so sure," declared Hollyer doubtfully. "There was a feeling of suspicion and—before me— polite hatred that would have gone a good way towards it. All the same there was something more definite. Millicent told me this the day after I went there. There is no doubt that a few months ago Creake deliberately planned to poison her with some weed-killer. She told me the circumstances in a rather distressed moment, but afterwards she refused to speak of it again—even weakly denied it—and, as a matter of fact, it was with the greatest of difficulty that I could get her at any time to talk about her husband or his affairs. The gist of it was that she had the strongest suspicion that Creake doctored a bottle of stout which he expected she would drink for her supper when she was alone. The weed-killer, properly labelled, but also in a beer bottle, was kept with other miscellaneous liquids in the same cupboard as the beer but on a high shelf. When he found that it had miscarried he poured away the mixture, washed out the bottle and put in the dregs from another. There is no doubt in my mind that if he had come back and found Millicent dead or dying he would have contrived it to appear that she had made a mistake in the dark and drunk some of the poison before she found out."

"Yes," assented Carrados. "The open way; the safe way."

"You must understand that they live in a very small style, Mr. Carrados, and Millicent is almost entirely in the man's power. The only servant they have is a woman who comes in for a few hours every day. The house is lonely and secluded. Creake is sometimes away for days and nights at a time, and Millicent, either through pride or indifference, seems to have dropped off all her old friends and to have made no others. He might poison her, bury the body in the garden, and be a thousand miles away before anyone began even to inquire about her. What am I to do, Mr. Carrados?"

"He is less likely to try poison than some other means now," pondered Carrados. "That having failed, his wife will always be on her guard. He may know, or at least suspect, that others know. No. ... The common-sense precaution would be for your sister to leave the man, Mr. Hollyer. She will not?"

"No," admitted Hollyer, "she will not. I at once urged that." The young man struggled with some hesitation for a moment and then blurted out: "The fact is, Mr. Carrados, I don't understand Millicent. She is not the girl she was. She hates Creake and treats him with a silent contempt that eats into their lives like acid, and yet she is so jealous of him that she will let nothing short of death part them. It is a horrible life they lead. I stood it for a week and I must say, much as I dislike my brother-in-law, that he has something to put up with. If only he got into a passion like a man and killed her it wouldn't be altogether incomprehensible."

"That does not concern us," said Carrados. "In a game of this kind one has to take sides and we have taken ours. It remains for us to see that our side wins. You mentioned jealousy, Mr. Hollyer. Have you any idea whether Mrs. Creake has real ground for it?"

"I should have told you that," replied Lieutenant Hollyer. "I happened to strike up with a newspaper man whose office is in the same block as Creake's. When I mentioned the name he grinned. 'Creake,' he said, 'oh, he's the man with the romantic typist, isn't he?' 'Well, he's my brother-in-law,' I replied. 'What about the typist?' Then the chap shut up like a knife. 'No, no,' he said, 'I didn't know he was married. I don't want to get mixed up in anything of that sort. I only said that he had a typist. Well, what of that? So have we; so has everyone.' There was nothing more to be got out of him, but the remark and the grin meant—well, about as usual, Mr. Carrados."

Carrados turned to his friend.

"I suppose you know all about the typist by now, Louis?"

"We have had her under efficient observation, Max," replied Mr. Carlyle with severe dignity.

"Is she unmarried?"

"Yes; so far as ordinary repute goes, she is."

"That is all that is essential for the moment. Mr. Hollyer opens up three excellent reasons why this man might wish to dispose of his wife. If we accept the suggestion of poisoning—though we have only a jealous woman's suspicion for it—we add to the wish the determination. Well, we will go forward on that. Have you got a photograph of Mr. Creake?"

The lieutenant took out his pocket-book.

"Mr. Carlyle asked me for one. Here is the best I could get."

Carrados rang the bell.

"This, Parkinson," he said, when the man appeared, "is a photograph of a Mr. — What first name, by the way?"

"Austin," put in Hollyer, who was following everything with a boyish mixture of excitement and subdued importance.

"—of a Mr. Austin Creake. I may require you to recognize him."

Parkinson glanced at the print and returned it to his master's hand.

"May I inquire if it is a recent photograph of the gentleman, sir?" he asked.

"About six years ago," said the lieutenant, taking in this new actor in the drama with frank curiosity. "But he is very little changed."

"Thank you, sir. I will endeavour to remember Mr. Creake, sir."

Lieutenant Hollyer stood up as Parkinson left the room. The interview seemed to be at an end.

"Oh, there's one other matter," he remarked. "I am afraid that I did rather an unfortunate thing while I was at Brookbend. It seemed to me that as all Millicent's money would probably pass into Creake's hands sooner or later I might as well have my five hundred pounds, if only to help her with afterwards. So I broached the subject and said that I should like to have it now as I had an opportunity for investing."

"And you think?"

"It may possibly influence Creake to act sooner than he otherwise might have done. He may have got possession of the principal even and find it very awkward to replace it."

"So much the better. If your sister is going to be murdered it may as well be done next week as next year so far as I am concerned. Excuse my brutality, Mr. Hollyer, but this is simply a case to me and I regard it strategically. Now Mr. Carlyle's organization can look after Mrs. Creake for a few weeks, but it cannot look after her for ever. By increasing the immediate risk we diminish the permanent risk."

"I see," agreed Hollyer. "I'm awfully uneasy but I'm entirely in your hands."

"Then we will give Mr. Creake every inducement and every opportunity to get to work. Where are you staying now?"

"Just now with some friends at St. Albans."

"That is too far." The inscrutable eyes retained their tranquil depth but a new quality of quickening interest in the voice made Mr. Carlyle forget the weight and burden of his ruffled dignity. "Give me a few minutes, please. The cigarettes are behind you, Mr. Hollyer." The blind man walked to the window and seemed to look out over the cypress-shaded lawn. The lieutenant lit a cigarette and Mr. Carlyle picked up Punch. Then Carrados turned round again.

"You are prepared to put your own arrangements aside?" he demanded of his visitor.

"Certainly."

"Very well. I want you to go down now—straight from here—to Brookbend Cottage. Tell your sister that your leave is unexpectedly cut short and that you sail to-morrow."

"The Martian?'

"No, no; the Martian doesn't sail. Look up the movements on your way there and pick out a boat that does. Say you are transferred. Add that you expect to be away only two or three months and that you really want the five hundred pounds by the time of your return. Don't stay in the house long, please."

"I understand, sir."

"St. Albans is too far. Make your excuse and get away from there to-day. Put up somewhere in town, where you will be in reach of the telephone. Let Mr. Carlyle and myself know where you are. Keep out of Creake's way. I don't want actually to tie you down to the house, but we may require your services. We will let you know at the first sign of anything doing and if there is nothing to be done we must release you."

"I don't mind that. Is there nothing more that I can do now?"

"Nothing. In going to Mr. Carlyle you have done the best thing possible; you have put your sister into the care of the shrewdest man in London." Whereat the object of this quite unexpected eulogy found himself becoming covered with modest confusion.

"Well, Max?" remarked Mr. Carlyle tentatively when they were alone.

"Well, Louis?"

"Of course it wasn't worth while rubbing it in before young Hollyer, but, as a matter of fact, every single man carries the life of any other man—only one, mind you—in his hands, do what you will."

"Provided he doesn't bungle," acquiesced Carrados.

"Quite so."

"And also that he is absolutely reckless of the consequences."

"Of course."

"Two rather large provisos. Creake is obviously susceptible to both. Have you seen him?"

"No. As I told you, I put a man on to report his habits in town. Then, two days ago, as the case seemed to promise some interest—for he certainly is deeply involved with the typist, Max, and the thing might take a sensational turn at any time—I went down to Mulling Common myself. Although the house is lonely it is on the electric tram route. You know the sort of market garden rurality that about a dozen miles out of London offers—alternate bricks and cabbages. It was easy enough to get to know about Creake locally. He mixes with no one there, goes into town at irregular times but generally every day, and is reputed to be devilish hard to get money out of. Finally I made the acquaintance of an old fellow who used to do a day's gardening at Brookbend occasionally. He has a cottage and a garden of his own with a greenhouse, and the business cost me the price of a pound of tomatoes."

"Was it—a profitable investment?"

"As tomatoes, yes; as information, no. The old fellow had the fatal disadvantage from our point of view of labouring under a grievance. A few weeks ago Creake told him that he would not require him again as he was going to do his own gardening in future."

"That is something, Louis."

"If only Creake was going to poison his wife with hyoscyamine and bury her, instead of blowing her up with a dynamite cartridge and claiming that it came in among the coal."

"True, true. Still—"

"However, the chatty old soul had a simple explanation for everything that Creake did. Creake was mad. He had even seen him flying a kite in his garden where it was found to get wrecked among the trees. A lad of ten would have known better, he declared. And certainly the kite did get wrecked, for I saw it hanging over the road myself. But that a sane man should spend his time 'playing with a toy' was beyond him."

"A good many men have been flying kites of various kinds lately," said Carrados. "Is he interested in aviation?"

"I dare say. He appears to have some knowledge of scientific subjects. Now what do you want me to do, Max?"

"Will you do it?"

"Implicitly—subject to the usual reservations."

"Keep your man on Creake in town and let me have his reports after you have seen them. Lunch with me here now. 'Phone up to your office that you are detained on unpleasant business and then give the deserving Parkinson an afternoon off by looking after me while we take a motor run round Mulling Common. If we have time we might go on to Brighton, feed at the 'Ship,' and come back in the cool."

"Amiable and thrice lucky mortal," sighed Mr. Carlyle, his glance wandering round the room.

But, as it happened, Brighton did not figure in that day's itinerary. It had been Carrados's intention merely to pass Brookbend Cottage on this occasion, relying on his highly developed faculties, aided by Mr. Carlyle's description, to inform him of the surroundings. A hundred yards before they reached the house he had given an order to his chauffeur to drop into the lowest speed and they were leisurely drawing past when a discovery by Mr. Carlyle modified their plans.

"By Jupiter!" that gentleman suddenly exclaimed, "there's a board up, Max. The place is to be let."

Carrados picked up the tube again. A couple of sentences passed and the car stopped by the roadside, a score of paces past the limit of the garden. Mr. Carlyle took out his notebook and wrote down the address of a firm of house agents.

"You might raise the bonnet and have a look at the engines, Harris," said Carrados. "We want to be occupied here for a few minutes."

"This is sudden; Hollyer knew nothing of their leaving," remarked Mr. Carlyle.

"Probably not for three months yet. All the same, Louis, we will go on to the agents and get a card to view whether we use it to-day or not."

A thick hedge, in its summer dress effectively screening the house beyond from public view, lay between the garden and the road. Above the hedge showed an occasional shrub; at the corner nearest to the car a chestnut flourished. The wooden gate, once white, which they had passed, was grimed and rickety. The road itself was still the unpretentious country lane that the advent of the electric car had found it. When Carrados had taken in these details there seemed little else to notice. He was on the point of giving Harris the order to go on when his ear caught a trivial sound.

"Someone is coming out of the house, Louis," he warned his friend. "It may be Hollyer, but he ought to have gone by this time."

"I don't hear anyone," replied the other, but as he spoke a door banged noisily and Mr. Carlyle slipped into another seat and ensconced himself behind a copy of The Globe.

"Creake himself," he whispered across the car, as a man appeared at the gate. "Hollyer was right; he is hardly changed. Waiting for a car, I suppose."

But a car very soon swung past them from the direction in which Mr. Creake was looking and it did not interest him. For a minute or two longer he continued to look expectantly along the road. Then he walked slowly up the drive back to the house.

"We will give him five or ten minutes," decided Carrados. "Harris is behaving very naturally."

Before even the shorter period had run out they were repaid. A telegraph-boy cycled leisurely along the road, and, leaving his machine at the gate, went up to the cottage. Evidently there was no reply, for in less than a minute he was trundling past them back again. Round the bend an approaching tram clanged its bell noisily, and, quickened by the warning sound, Mr. Creake again appeared, this time with a small portmanteau in his hand. With a backward glance he hurried on towards the next stopping-place, and, boarding the car as it slackened down, he was carried out of their knowledge.

"Very convenient of Mr. Creake," remarked Carrados, with quiet satisfaction. "We will now get the order and go over the house in his absence. It might be useful to have a look at the wire as well."

"It might, Max," acquiesced Mr. Carlyle a little dryly. "But if it is, as it probably is in Creake's pocket, how do you propose to get it?"

"By going to the post office, Louis."

"Quite so. Have you ever tried to see a copy of a telegram addressed to someone else?"

"I don't think I have ever had occasion yet," admitted Carrados. "Have you?"

"In one or two cases I have perhaps been an accessory to the act. It is generally a matter either of extreme delicacy or considerable expenditure."

"Then for Hollyer's sake we will hope for the former here." And Mr. Carlyle smiled darkly and hinted that he was content to wait for a friendly revenge.

A little later, having left the car at the beginning of the straggling High Street, the two men called at the village post office. They had already visited the house agent and obtained an order to view Brookbend Cottage, declining with some difficulty the clerk's persistent offer to accompany them. The reason was soon forthcoming. "As a matter of fact," explained the young man, "the present tenant is under our notice to leave."

"Unsatisfactory, eh?" said Carrados encouragingly.

"He's a corker," admitted the clerk, responding to the friendly tone. "Fifteen months and not a doit of rent have we had. That's why I should have liked—"

"We will make every allowance," replied Carrados.

The post office occupied one side of a stationer's shop. It was not without some inward trepidation that Mr. Carlyle found himself committed to the adventure. Carrados, on the other hand, was the personification of bland unconcern.

"You have just sent a telegram to Brookbend Cottage," he said to the young lady behind the brasswork lattice. "We think it may have come inaccurately and should like a repeat." He took out his purse. "What is the fee?"

The request was evidently not a common one. "Oh," said the girl uncertainly, "wait a minute, please." She turned to a pile of telegram duplicates behind the desk and ran a doubtful finger along the upper sheets. "I think this is all right. You want it repeated?"

"Please." Just a tinge of questioning surprise gave point to the courteous tone.

"It will be fourpence. If there is an error the amount will be refunded."

Carrados put down his coin and received his change.

"Will it take long?" he inquired carelessly, as he pulled on his glove.

"You will most likely get it within a quarter of an hour," she replied.

"Now you've done it," commented Mr. Carlyle as they walked back to their car. "How do you propose to get that telegram, Max?"

"Ask for it," was the laconic explanation.

And, stripping the artifice of any elaboration, he simply asked for it and got it. The car, posted at a convenient bend in the road, gave him a warning note as the telegraph-boy approached. Then Carrados took up a convincing attitude with his hand on the gate while Mr. Carlyle lent himself to the semblance of a departing friend. That was the inevitable impression when the boy rode up.

"Creake, Brookbend Cottage?" inquired Carrados, holding out his hand, and without a second thought the boy gave him the envelope and rode away on the assurance that there would be no reply.

"Some day, my friend," remarked Mr. Carlyle, looking nervously toward the unseen house, "your ingenuity will get you into a tight corner."

"Then my ingenuity must get me out again," was the retort. "Let us have our 'view' now. The telegram can wait."

An untidy workwoman took their order and left them standing at the door. Presently a lady whom they both knew to be Mrs. Creake appeared.

"You wish to see over the house?" she said, in a voice that was utterly devoid of any interest. Then, without waiting for a reply, she turned to the nearest door and threw it open.

"This is the drawing-room," she said, standing aside.

They walked into a sparsely furnished, damp-smelling room and made a pretence of looking round, while Mrs. Creake remained silent and aloof.

"The dining-room," she continued, crossing the narrow hall and opening another door.

Mr. Carlyle ventured a genial commonplace in the hope of inducing conversation. The result was not encouraging. Doubtless they would have gone through the house under the same frigid guidance had not Carrados been at fault in a way that Mr. Carlyle had never known him fail before. In crossing the hall he stumbled over a mat and almost fell.

"Pardon my clumsiness," he said to the lady. "I am, unfortunately, quite blind. But," he added, with a smile, to turn off the mishap, "even a blind man must have a house."

The man who had eyes was surprised to see a flood of colour rush into Mrs. Creake's face.

"Blind!" she exclaimed, "oh, I beg your pardon. Why did you not tell me? You might have fallen."

"I generally manage fairly well," he replied. "But, of course, in a strange house—"

She put her hand on his arm very lightly.

"You must let me guide you, just a little," she said.

The house, without being large, was full of passages and inconvenient turnings. Carrados asked an occasional question and found Mrs. Creake quite amiable without effusion. Mr. Carlyle followed them from room to room in the hope, though scarcely the expectation, of learning something that might be useful.

"This is the last one. It is the largest bedroom," said their guide. Only two of the upper rooms were fully furnished and Mr. Carlyle at once saw, as Carrados knew without seeing, that this was the one which the Creakes occupied.

"A very pleasant outlook," declared Mr. Carlyle.

"Oh, I suppose so," admitted the lady vaguely. The room, in fact, looked over the leafy garden and the road beyond. It had a French window opening on to a small balcony, and to this, under the strange influence that always attracted him to light, Carrados walked.

"I expect that there is a certain amount of repair needed?" he said, after standing there a moment.

"I am afraid there would be," she confessed.

"I ask because there is a sheet of metal on the floor here," he continued. "Now that, in an old house, spells dry rot to the wary observer."

"My husband said that the rain, which comes in a little under the window, was rotting the boards there," she replied. "He put that down recently. I had not noticed anything myself."

It was the first time she had mentioned her husband; Mr. Carlyle pricked up his ears.

"Ah, that is a less serious matter," said Carrados. "May I step out on to the balcony?"

"Oh yes, if you like to." Then, as he appeared to be fumbling at the catch, "Let me open it for you."

But the window was already open, and Carrados, facing the various points of the compass, took in the bearings.

"A sunny, sheltered corner," he remarked. "An ideal spot for a deck-chair and a book."

She shrugged her shoulders half contemptuously.

"I dare say," she replied, "but I never use it."

"Sometimes, surely," he persisted mildly. "It would be my favourite retreat. But then—"

"I was going to say that I had never even been out on it, but that would not be quite true. It has two uses for me, both equally romantic; I occasionally shake a duster from it, and when my husband returns late without his latchkey he wakes me up and I come out here and drop him mine."

Further revelation of Mr. Creake's nocturnal habits was cut off, greatly to Mr. Carlyle's annoyance, by a cough of unmistakable significance from the foot of the stairs. They had heard a trade cart drive up to the gate, a knock at the door, and the heavy-footed woman tramp along the hall.

"Excuse me a minute, please," said Mrs. Creake.

"Louis," said Carrados, in a sharp whisper, the moment they were alone, "stand against the door."

With extreme plausibility Mr. Carlyle began to admire a picture so situated that while he was there it was impossible to open the door more than a few inches. From that position he observed his confederate go through the curious procedure of kneeling down on the bedroom floor and for a full minute pressing his ear to the sheet of metal that had already engaged his attention. Then he rose to his feet, nodded, dusted his trousers, and Mr. Carlyle moved to a less equivocal position.

"What a beautiful rose-tree grows up your balcony," remarked Carrados, stepping into the room as Mrs. Creake returned. "I suppose you are very fond of gardening?"

"I detest it," she replied.

"But this Gloire, so carefully trained—?"

"Is it?" she replied. "I think my husband was nailing it up recently." By some strange fatality Carrados's most aimless remarks seemed to involve the absent Mr. Creake. "Do you care to see the garden?"

The garden proved to be extensive and neglected. Behind the house was chiefly orchard. In front, some semblance of order had been kept up; here it was lawn and shrubbery, and the drive they had walked along. Two things interested Carrados: the soil at the foot of the balcony, which he declared on examination to be particularly suitable for roses, and the fine chestnut-tree in the corner by the road.

As they walked back to the car Mr. Carlyle lamented that they had learned so little of Creake's movements.

"Perhaps the telegram will tell us something," suggested Carrados. "Read it, Louis."

Mr. Carlyle cut open the envelope, glanced at the enclosure, and in spite of his disappointment could not restrain a chuckle.

"My poor Max," he explained, "you have put yourself to an amount of ingenious trouble for nothing. Creake is evidently taking a few days' holiday and prudently availed himself of the Meteorological Office forecast before going. Listen: 'Immediate prospect for London warm and settled. Further outlook cooler but fine.' Well, well; I did get a pound of tomatoes for my fourpence."

"You certainly scored there, Louis," admitted Carrados, with humorous appreciation. "I wonder," he added speculatively, "whether it is Creake's peculiar taste usually to spend his week-end holiday in London."

"Eh?" exclaimed Mr. Carlyle, looking at the words again, "by gad, that's rum, Max. They go to Weston-super-Mare. Why on earth should he want to know about London?"

"I can make a guess, but before we are satisfied I must come here again. Take another look at that kite, Louis. Are there a few yards of string hanging loose from it?"

"Yes, there are."

"Rather thick string—unusually thick for the purpose?"

"Yes, but how do you know?"

As they drove home again Carrados explained, and Mr. Carlyle sat aghast, saying incredulously: "Good God, Max, is it possible?"

An hour later he was satisfied that it was possible. In reply to his inquiry someone in his office telephoned him the information that "they" had left Paddington by the four-thirty for Weston.

It was more than a week after his introduction to Carrados that Lieutenant Hollyer had a summons to present himself at The Turrets again. He found Mr. Carlyle already there and the two friends were awaiting his arrival.

"I stayed in all day after hearing from you this morning, Mr. Carrados," he said, shaking hands. "When I got your second message I was all ready to walk straight out of the house. That's how I did it in the time. I hope everything is all right?"

"Excellent," replied Carrados. "You'd better have something before we start. We probably have a long and perhaps an exciting night before us."

"And certainly a wet one," assented the lieutenant. "It was thundering over Mulling way as I came along."

"That is why you are here," said his host. "We are waiting for a certain message before we start, and in the meantime you may as well understand what we expect to happen. As you saw, there is a thunderstorm coming on. The Meteorological Office morning forecast predicted it for the whole of London if the conditions remained. That is why I kept you in readiness. Within an hour it is now inevitable that we shall experience a deluge. Here and there damage will be done to trees and buildings; here and there a person will probably be struck and killed."

"Yes."

"It is Mr. Creake's intention that his wife should be among the victims."

"I don't exactly follow," said Hollyer, looking from one man to the other. "I quite admit that Creake would be immensely relieved if such a thing did happen, but the chance is surely an absurdly remote one."

"Yet unless we intervene it is precisely what a coroner's jury will decide has happened. Do you know whether your brother-in-law has any practical knowledge of electricity, Mr. Hollyer?"

"I cannot say. He was so reserved, and we really knew so little of him—"

"Yet in 1896 an Austin Creake contributed an article on 'Alternating Currents' to the American Scientific World. That would argue a fairly intimate acquaintanceship."

"But do you mean that he is going to direct a flash of lightning?"

"Only into the minds of the doctor who conducts the post-mortem, and the coroner. This storm, the opportunity for which he has been waiting for weeks, is merely the cloak to his act. The weapon which he has planned to use—scarcely less powerful than lightning but much more tractable—is the high voltage current of electricity that flows along the tram wire at his gate."

"Oh!" exclaimed Lieutenant Hollyer, as the sudden revelation struck him.

"Some time between eleven o'clock to-night—about the hour when your sister goes to bed—and one thirty in the morning—the time up to which he can rely on the current—Creake will throw a stone up at the balcony window. Most of his preparation has long been made; it only remains for him to connect up a short length to the window handle and a longer one at the other end to tap the live wire. That done, he will wake his wife in the way I have said. The moment she moves the catch of the window—and he has carefully filed its parts to ensure perfect contact—she will be electrocuted as effectually as if she sat in the executioner's chair in Sing Sing prison."

"But what are we doing here!" exclaimed Hollyer, starting to his feet, pale and horrified. "It is past ten now and anything may happen."

"Quite natural, Mr. Hollyer," said Carrados reassuringly, "but you need have no anxiety. Creake is being watched, the house is being watched, and your sister is as safe as if she slept to-night in Windsor Castle. Be assured that whatever happens he will not be allowed to complete his scheme; but it is desirable to let him implicate himself to the fullest limit. Your brother-in-law, Mr. Hollyer, is a man with a peculiar capacity for taking pains."

"He is a damned cold-blooded scoundrel!" exclaimed the young officer fiercely. "When I think of Millicent five years ago—"

"Well, for that matter, an enlightened nation has decided that electrocution is the most humane way of removing its superfluous citizens," suggested Carrados mildly. "He is certainly an ingenious-minded gentleman. It is his misfortune that in Mr. Carlyle he was fated to be opposed by an even subtler brain—"

"No, no! Really, Max!" protested the embarrassed gentleman.

"Mr. Hollyer will be able to judge for himself when I tell him that it was Mr. Carlyle who first drew attention to the significance of the abandoned kite," insisted Carrados firmly. "Then, of course, its object became plain to me—as indeed to anyone. For ten minutes, perhaps, a wire must be carried from the overhead line to the chestnut-tree. Creake has everything in his favour, but it is just within possibility that the driver of an inopportune train might notice the appendage. What of that? Why, for more than a week he has seen a derelict kite with its yards of trailing string hanging in the tree. A very calculating mind, Mr. Hollyer. It would be interesting to know what line of action Mr. Creake has mapped out for himself afterwards. I expect he has half-a-dozen artistic little touches up his sleeve. Possibly he would merely singe his wife's hair, burn her feet with a red-hot poker, shiver the glass of the French window, and be content with that to let well alone. You see, lightning is so varied in its effects that whatever he did or did not do would be right. He is in the impregnable position of the body showing all the symptoms of death by lightning shock and nothing else but lightning to account for it—a dilated eye, heart contracted in systole, bloodless lungs shrunk to a third the normal weight, and all the rest of it. When he has removed a few outward traces of his work Creake might quite safely 'discover' his dead wife and rush off for the nearest doctor. Or he may have decided to arrange a convincing alibi, and creep away, leaving the discovery to another. We shall never know; he will make no confession."

"I wish it was well over," admitted Hollyer, "I'm not particularly jumpy, but this gives me a touch of the creeps."

"Three more hours at the worst, lieutenant," said Carrados cheerfully. "Ah-ha, something is coming through now."

He went to the telephone and received a message from one quarter; then made another connection and talked for a few minutes with someone else.

"Everything working smoothly," he remarked between times over his shoulder. "Your sister has gone to bed, Mr. Hollyer."

Then he turned to the house telephone and distributed his orders.

"So we," he concluded, "must get up."

By the time they were ready a large closed motor car was waiting. The lieutenant thought he recognised Parkinson in the well-swathed form beside the driver, but there was no temptation to linger for a second on the steps. Already the stinging rain had lashed the drive into the semblance of a frothy estuary; all round the lightning jagged its course through the incessant tremulous glow of more distant lightning, while the thunder only ceased its muttering to turn at close quarters and crackle viciously.

"One of the few things I regret missing," remarked Carrados tranquilly; "but I hear a good deal of colour in it."

The car slushed its way down to the gate, lurched a little heavily across the dip into the road, and, steadying as it came upon the straight, began to hum contentedly along the deserted highway.

"We are not going direct?" suddenly inquired Hollyer, after they had travelled perhaps half-a-dozen miles. The night was bewildering enough but he had the sailor's gift for location.

"No; through Hunscott Green and then by a field-path to the orchard at the back," replied Carrados. "Keep a sharp look out for the man with the lantern about here, Harris," he called through the tube.

"Something flashing just ahead, sir," came the reply, and the car slowed down and stopped.

Carrados dropped the near window as a man in glistening waterproof stepped from the shelter of a lich-gate and approached.

"Inspector Beedel, sir," said the stranger, looking into the car.

"Quite right, Inspector," said Carrados. "Get in."

"I have a man with me, sir."

"We can find room for him as well."

"We are very wet."

"So shall we all be soon."

The lieutenant changed his seat and the two burly forms took places side by side. In less than five minutes the car stopped again, this time in a grassy country lane.

"Now we have to face it," announced Carrados. "The inspector will show us the way."

The car slid round and disappeared into the night, while Beedel led the party to a stile in the hedge. A couple of fields brought them to the Brookbend boundary. There a figure stood out of the black foliage, exchanged a few words with their guide and piloted them along the shadows of the orchard to the back door of the house.

"You will find a broken pane near the catch of the scullery window," said the blind man.

"Right, sir," replied the inspector. "I have it. Now who goes through?"

"Mr. Hollyer will open the door for us. I'm afraid you must take off your boots and all wet things, Lieutenant. We cannot risk a single spot inside."

They waited until the back door opened, then each one divested himself in a similar manner and passed into the kitchen, where the remains of a fire still burned. The man from the orchard gathered together the discarded garments and disappeared again.

Carrados turned to the lieutenant.

"A rather delicate job for you now, Mr. Hollyer. I want you to go up to your sister, wake her, and get her into another room with as little fuss as possible. Tell her as much as you think fit and let her understand that her very life depends on absolute stillness when she is alone. Don't be unduly hurried, but not a glimmer of a light, please."

Ten minutes passed by the measure of the battered old alarum on the dresser shelf before the young man returned.

"I've had rather a time of it," he reported, with a nervous laugh, "but I think it will be all right now. She is in the spare room."

"Then we will take our places. You and Parkinson come with me to the bedroom. Inspector, you have your own arrangements. Mr. Carlyle will be with you."

They dispersed silently about the house. Hollyer glanced apprehensively at the door of the spare room as they passed it, but within was as quiet as the grave. Their room lay at the other end of the passage.

"You may as well take your place in the bed now, Hollyer," directed Carrados when they were inside and the door closed. "Keep well down among the clothes. Creake has to get up on the balcony, you know, and he will probably peep through the window, but he dare come no farther. Then when he begins to throw up stones slip on this dressing-gown of your sister's. I'll tell you what to do after."

The next sixty minutes drew out into the longest hour that the lieutenant had ever known. Occasionally he heard a whisper pass between the two men who stood behind the window curtains, but he could see nothing. Then Carrados threw a guarded remark in his direction.

"He is in the garden now."

Something scraped slightly against the outer wall. But the night was full of wilder sounds, and in the house the furniture and the boards creaked and sprung between the yawling of the wind among the chimneys, the rattle of the thunder and the pelting of the rain. It was a time to quicken the steadiest pulse, and when the crucial moment came, when a pebble suddenly rang against the pane with a sound that the tense waiting magnified into a shivering crash, Hollyer leapt from the bed on the instant.

"Easy, easy," warned Carrados feelingly. "We will wait for another knock." He passed something across. "Here is a rubber glove. I have cut the wire but you had better put it on. Stand just for a moment at the window, move the catch so that it can blow open a little, and drop immediately. Now."

Another stone had rattled against the glass. For Hollyer to go through his part was the work merely of seconds, and with a few touches Carrados spread the dressing-gown to more effective disguise about the extended form. But an unforeseen and in the circumstances rather horrible interval followed, for Creake, in accordance with some detail of his never-revealed plan, continued to shower missile after missile against the panes until even the unimpressionable Parkinson shivered.

"The last act," whispered Carrados, a moment after the throwing had ceased. "He has gone round to the back. Keep as you are. We take cover now." He pressed behind the arras of an extemporized wardrobe, and the spirit of emptiness and desolation seemed once more to reign over the lonely house.

From half-a-dozen places of concealment ears were straining to catch the first guiding sound. He moved very stealthily, burdened, perhaps, by some strange scruple in the presence of the tragedy that he had not feared to contrive, paused for a moment at the bedroom door, then opened it very quietly, and in the fickle light read the consummation of his hopes.

"At last!" they heard the sharp whisper drawn from his relief. "At last!"

He took another step and two shadows seemed to fall upon him from behind, one on either side. With primitive instinct a cry of terror and surprise escaped him as he made a desperate movement to wrench himself free, and for a short second he almost succeeded in dragging one hand into a pocket. Then his wrists slowly came together and the handcuffs closed.

"I am Inspector Beedel," said the man on his right side. "You are charged with the attempted murder of your wife, Millicent Creake."

"You are mad," retorted the miserable creature, falling into a desperate calmness. "She has been struck by lightning."

"No, you blackguard, she hasn't," wrathfully exclaimed his brother-in-law, jumping up. "Would you like to see her?"

"I also have to warn you," continued the inspector impassively, "that anything you say may be used as evidence against you."

A startled cry from the farther end of the passage arrested their attention.

"Mr. Carrados," called Hollyer, "oh, come at once."

At the open door of the other bedroom stood the lieutenant, his eyes still turned towards something in the room beyond, a little empty bottle in his hand.

"Dead!" he exclaimed tragically, with a sob, "with this beside her. Dead just when she would have been free of the brute."

The blind man passed into the room, sniffed the air, and laid a gentle hand on the pulseless heart.

"Yes," he replied. "That, Hollyer, does not always appeal to the woman, strange to say."

THE LAST EXPLOIT OF HARRY THE ACTOR

The one insignificant fact upon which turned the following incident in the joint experiences of Mr. Carlyle and Max Carrados was merely this: that having called upon his friend just at the moment when the private detective was on the point of leaving his office to go to the safe deposit in Lucas Street, Piccadilly, the blind amateur accompanied him, and for ten minutes amused himself by sitting quite quietly among the palms in the centre of the circular hall while Mr. Carlyle was occupied with his deed-box in one of the little compartments provided for the purpose.

The Lucas Street depository was then (it has since been converted into a picture palace) generally accepted as being one of the strongest places in London. The front of the building was constructed to represent a gigantic safe door, and under the colloquial designation of "The Safe" the place had passed into a synonym for all that was secure and impregnable. Half of the marketable securities in the west of London were popularly reported to have seen the inside of its coffers at one time or another, together with the same generous proportion of family jewels. However exaggerated an estimate this might be, the substratum of truth was solid and auriferous enough to dazzle the imagination. When ordinary safes were being carried bodily away with impunity or ingeniously fused open by the scientifically equipped cracksman, nervous bond-holders turned with relief to the attractions of an establishment whose modest claim was summed up in its telegraphic address: "Impregnable." To it went also the jewel-case between the lady's social engagements, and when in due course "the family" journeyed north—or south, east or west—whenever, in short, the London house was closed, its capacious storerooms received the plate-chest as an established custom. Not a few traders also—jewellers, financiers, dealers in pictures, antiques and costly bijouterie, for instance—constantly used its facilities for any stock that they did not require immediately to hand.

There was only one entrance to the place, an exaggerated keyhole, to carry out the similitude of the safe-door alluded to. The ground floor was occupied by the ordinary offices of the company; all the strong-rooms and safes lay in the steel-cased basement. This was reached both by a lift and by a flight of steps. In either case the visitor found before him a grille of massive proportions. Behind its bars stood a formidable commissionaire who never left his post, his sole duty being to open and close the grille to arriving and departing clients. Beyond this, a short passage led into the round central hall where Carrados was waiting. From this part, other passages radiated off to the vaults and strong-rooms, each one barred from the hall by a grille scarcely less ponderous than the first one. The doors of the various private rooms put at the disposal of the company's clients, and that of the manager's office, filled the wall-space between the radiating passages. Everything was very quiet, everything looked very bright, and everything seemed hopelessly impregnable.

"But I wonder?" ran Carrados's dubious reflection as he reached this point.

"Sorry to have kept you so long, my dear Max," broke in Mr. Carlyle's crisp voice. He had emerged from his compartment and was crossing the hall, deed-box in hand. "Another minute and I will be with you."

Carrados smiled and nodded and resumed his former expression, which was merely that of an uninterested gentleman waiting patiently for another. It is something of an attainment to watch closely without betraying undue curiosity, but others of the senses—hearing and smelling, for instance—can be keenly engaged while the observer possibly has the appearance of falling asleep.

"Now," announced Mr. Carlyle, returning briskly to his friend's chair, and drawing on his grey suède gloves.

"You are in no particular hurry?"

"No," admitted the professional man, with the slowness of mild surprise. "Not at all. What do you propose?"

"It is very pleasant here," replied Carrados tranquilly. "Very cool and restful with this armoured steel between us and the dust and scurry of the hot July afternoon above. I propose remaining here for a few minutes longer."

"Certainly," agreed Mr. Carlyle, taking the nearest chair and eyeing Carrados as though he had a shrewd suspicion of something more than met the ear. "I believe some very interesting people rent safes here. We may encounter a bishop, or a winning jockey, or even a musical comedy actress. Unfortunately it seems to be rather a slack time."

"Two men came down while you were in your cubicle," remarked Carrados casually. "The first took the lift. I imagine that he was a middle-aged, rather portly man. He carried a stick, wore a silk hat, and used spectacles for close sight. The other came by the stairway. I infer that he arrived at the top immediately after the lift had gone. He ran down the steps, so that the two were admitted at the same time, but the second man, though the more active of the pair, hung back for a moment in the passage and the portly one was the first to go to his safe."

Mr. Carlyle's knowing look expressed: "Go on, my friend; you are coming to something." But he merely contributed an encouraging "Yes?"

"When you emerged just now our second man quietly opened the door of his pen a fraction. Doubtless he looked out. Then he closed it as quietly again. You were not his man, Louis."

"I am grateful," said Mr. Carlyle expressively. "What next, Max?"

"That is all; they are still closeted."

Both were silent for a moment. Mr. Carlyle's feeling was one of unconfessed perplexity. So far the incident was utterly trivial in his eyes; but he knew that the trifles which appeared significant to Max had a way of standing out like signposts when the time came to look back over an episode. Carrados's sightless faculties seemed indeed to keep him just a move ahead as the game progressed.

"Is there really anything in it, Max?" he asked at length.

"Who can say?" replied Carrados. "At least we may wait to see them go. Those tin deed-boxes now. There is one to each safe, I think?"

"Yes, so I imagine. The practice is to carry the box to your private lair and there unlock it and do your business. Then you lock it up again and take it back to your safe."

"Steady! our first man," whispered Carrados hurriedly. "Here, look at this with me." He opened a paper—a prospectus—which he pulled from his pocket, and they affected to study its contents together.

"You were about right, my friend," muttered Mr. Carlyle, pointing to a paragraph of assumed interest. "Hat, stick and spectacles. He is a clean-shaven, pink-faced old boy. I believe—yes, I know the man by sight. He is a bookmaker in a large way, I am told."

"Here comes the other," whispered Carrados.

The bookmaker passed across the hall, joined on his way by the manager whose duty it was to counterlock the safe, and disappeared along one of the passages. The second man sauntered up and down, waiting his turn. Mr. Carlyle reported his movements in an undertone and described him. He was a younger man than the other, of medium height, and passably well dressed in a quiet lounge suit, green Alpine hat and brown shoes. By the time the detective had reached his wavy chestnut hair, large and rather ragged moustache, and sandy, freckled complexion, the first man had completed his business and was leaving the place.

"It isn't an exchange lay, at all events," said Mr. Carlyle. "His inner case is only half the size of the other and couldn't possibly be substituted."

"Come up now," said Carrados, rising. "There is nothing more to be learned down here."

They requisitioned the lift, and on the steps outside the gigantic keyhole stood for a few minutes discussing an investment as a couple of trustees or a lawyer and a client who were parting there might do. Fifty yards away, a very large silk hat with a very curly brim marked the progress of the bookmaker towards Piccadilly.

The lift in the hall behind them swirled up again and the gate clashed. The second man walked leisurely out and sauntered away without a backward glance.

"He has gone in the opposite direction," exclaimed Mr. Carlyle, rather blankly. "It isn't the 'lame goat' nor the 'follow-me-on,' nor even the homely but efficacious sand-bag."

"What colour were his eyes?" asked Carrados.

"Upon my word, I never noticed," admitted the other.

"Parkinson would have noticed," was the severe comment.

"I am not Parkinson," retorted Mr. Carlyle, with asperity, "and, strictly as one dear friend to another, Max, permit me to add, that while cherishing an unbounded admiration for your remarkable gifts, I have the strongest suspicion that the whole incident is a ridiculous mare's nest, bred in the fantastic imagination of an enthusiastic criminologist."

Mr. Carrados received this outburst with the utmost benignity. "Come and have a coffee, Louis," he suggested. "Mehmed's is only a street away."

Mehmed proved to be a cosmopolitan gentleman from Mocha whose shop resembled a house from the outside and an Oriental divan when one was within. A turbaned Arab placed cigarettes and cups of coffee spiced with saffron before the customers, gave salaam and withdrew.

"You know, my dear chap," continued Mr. Carlyle, sipping his black coffee and wondering privately whether it was really very good or very bad, "speaking quite seriously, the one fishy detail—our ginger friend's watching for the other to leave—may be open to a dozen very innocent explanations."

"So innocent that to-morrow I intend taking a safe myself."

"You think that everything is all right?"

"On the contrary, I am convinced that something is very wrong."

"Then why—?"

"I shall keep nothing there, but it will give me the entrée. I should advise you, Louis, in the first place to empty your safe with all possible speed, and in the second to leave your business card on the manager."

Mr. Carlyle pushed his cup away, convinced now that the coffee was really very bad.

"But, my dear Max, the place—'The Safe'—is impregnable!"

"When I was in the States, three years ago, the head porter at one hotel took pains to impress on me that the building was absolutely fireproof. I at once had my things taken off to another hotel. Two weeks later the first place was burnt out. It was fireproof, I believe, but of course the furniture and the fittings were not and the walls gave way."

"Very ingenious," admitted Mr. Carlyle, "but why did you really go? You know you can't humbug me with your superhuman sixth sense, my friend."

Carrados smiled pleasantly, thereby encouraging the watchful attendant to draw near and replenish their tiny cups.

"Perhaps," replied the blind man, "because so many careless people were satisfied that it was fireproof."

"Ah-ha, there you are—the greater the confidence the greater the risk. But only if your self-confidence results in carelessness. Now do you know how this place is secured, Max?"

"I am told that they lock the door at night," replied Carrados, with bland malice.

"And hide the key under the mat to be ready for the first arrival in the morning," crowed Mr. Carlyle, in the same playful spirit. "Dear old chap! Well, let me tell you—"

"That force is out of the question. Quite so," admitted his friend.

"That simplifies the argument. Let us consider fraud. There again the precautions are so rigid that many people pronounce the forms a nuisance. I confess that I do not. I regard them as a means of protecting my own property and I cheerfully sign my name and give my password, which the manager compares with his record-book before he releases the first lock of my safe. The signature is burned before my eyes in a sort of crucible there, the password is of my own choosing and is written only in a book that no one but the manager ever sees, and my key is the sole one in existence."

"No duplicate or master-key?"

"Neither. If a key is lost it takes a skilful mechanic half-a-day to cut his way in. Then you must remember that clients of a safe-deposit are not multitudinous. All are known more or less by sight to the officials there, and a stranger would receive close attention. Now, Max, by what combination of circumstances is a rogue to know my password, to be able to forge my signature, to possess himself of my key, and to resemble me personally? And, finally, how is he possibly to determine beforehand whether there is anything in my safe to repay so elaborate a plant?" Mr. Carlyle concluded in triumph and was so carried away by the strength of his position that he drank off the contents of his second cup before he realized what he was doing.

"At the hotel I just spoke of," replied Carrados, "there was an attendant whose one duty in case of alarm was to secure three iron doors. On the night of the fire he had a bad attack of toothache and slipped away for just a quarter of an hour to have the thing out. There was a most up-to-date system of automatic fire alarm; it had been tested only the day before and the electrician, finding some part not absolutely to his satisfaction, had taken it away and not had time to replace it. The night watchman, it turned out, had received leave to present himself a couple of hours later on that particular night, and the hotel fireman, whose duties he took over, had missed being notified. Lastly, there was a big riverside blaze at the same time and all the engines were down at the other end of the city."

Mr. Carlyle committed himself to a dubious monosyllable. Carrados leaned forward a little.

"All these circumstances formed a coincidence of pure chance. Is it not conceivable, Louis, that an even more remarkable series might be brought about by design?"

"Our tawny friend?"

"Possibly. Only he was not really tawny." Mr. Carlyle's easy attitude suddenly stiffened into rigid attention. "He wore a false moustache."

"He wore a false moustache!" repeated the amazed gentleman. "And you cannot see! No, really, Max, this is beyond the limit!"

"If only you would not trust your dear, blundering old eyes so implicitly you would get nearer that limit yourself," retorted Carrados. "The man carried a five-yard aura of spirit gum, emphasized by a warm, perspiring skin. That inevitably suggested one thing. I looked for further evidence of making-up and found it—these preparations all smell. The hair you described was characteristically that of a wig—worn long to hide the joining and made wavy to minimize the length. All these things are trifles. As yet we have not gone beyond the initial stage of suspicion. I will tell you another trifle. When this man retired to a compartment with his deed-box, he never even opened it. Possibly it contains a brick and a newspaper. He is only watching."

"Watching the bookmaker."

"True, but it may go far wider than that. Everything points to a plot of careful elaboration. Still, if you are satisfied—"

"I am quite satisfied," replied Mr. Carlyle gallantly. "I regard 'The Safe' almost as a national institution, and as such I have an implicit faith in its precautions against every kind of force or fraud." So far Mr. Carlyle's attitude had been suggestive of a rock, but at this point he took out his watch, hummed a little to pass the time, consulted his watch again, and continued: "I am afraid that there were one or two papers which I overlooked. It would perhaps save me coming again to-morrow if I went back now—"

"Quite so," acquiesced Carrados, with perfect gravity. "I will wait for you."

For twenty minutes he sat there, drinking an occasional tiny cup of boiled coffee and to all appearance placidly enjoying the quaint atmosphere which Mr. Mehmed had contrived to transplant from the shores of the Persian Gulf.

At the end of that period Carlyle returned, politely effusive about the time he had kept his friend waiting but otherwise bland and unassailable. Anyone with eyes might have noticed that he carried a parcel of about the same size and dimensions as the deed-box that fitted his safe.

The next day Carrados presented himself at the safe-deposit as an intending renter. The manager showed him over the vaults and strong-rooms, explaining the various precautions taken to render the guile or force of man impotent: the strength of the chilled-steel walls, the casing of electricity-resisting concrete, the stupendous isolation of the whole inner fabric on metal pillars so that the watchman, while inside the building, could walk above, below, and all round the outer walls of what was really—although it bore no actual relationship to the advertising device of the front—a monstrous safe; and, finally, the arrangement which would enable the basement to be flooded with steam within three minutes of an alarm. These details were public property. "The Safe" was a showplace and its directors held that no harm could come of displaying a strong hand.

Accompanied by the observant eyes of Parkinson, Carrados gave an adventurous but not a hopeful attention to these particulars. Submitting the problem of the tawny man to his own ingenuity, he was constantly putting before himself the question: How shall I set about robbing this place? and he had already dismissed force as impracticable. Nor, when it came to the consideration of fraud, did the simple but effective safeguards which Mr. Carlyle had specified seem to offer any loophole.

"As I am blind I may as well sign in the book," he suggested, when the manager passed him a gummed slip for the purpose. The precaution against one acquiring particulars of another client might well be deemed superfluous in his case.

But the manager did not fall into the trap.

"It is our invariable rule in all cases, sir," he replied courteously. "What word will you take?" Parkinson, it may be said, had been left in the hall.

"Suppose I happen to forget it? How do we proceed?"

"In that case I am afraid that I might have to trouble you to establish your identity," the manager explained. "It rarely happens."

"Then we will say 'Conspiracy.'"

The word was written down and the book closed.

"Here is your key, sir. If you will allow me—your key-ring—"

A week went by and Carrados was no nearer the absolute solution of the problem he had set himself. He had, indeed, evolved several ways by which the contents of the safes might be reached, some simple and desperate, hanging on the razor-edge of chance to fall this way or that; others more elaborate, safer on the whole, but more liable to break down at some point of their ingenious intricacy. And setting aside complicity on the part of the manager—a condition that Carrados had satisfied himself did not exist—they all depended on a relaxation of the forms by which security was assured. Carrados continued to have several occasions to visit the safe during the week, and he "watched" with a quiet persistence that was deadly in its scope. But from beginning to end there was no indication of slackness in the business-like methods of the place; nor during any of his visits did the "tawny man" appear in that or any other disguise. Another week passed; Mr. Carlyle was becoming inexpressibly waggish, and Carrados himself, although he did not abate a jot of his conviction, was compelled to bend to the realities of the situation. The manager, with the obstinacy of a conscientious man who had become obsessed with the pervading note of security, excused himself from discussing abstract methods of fraud. Carrados was not in a position to formulate a detailed charge; he withdrew from active investigation, content to await his time.

It came, to be precise, on a certain Friday morning, seventeen days after his first visit to "The Safe." Returning late on the Thursday night, he was informed that a man giving the name of Draycott had called to see him. Apparently the matter had been of some importance to the visitor for he had returned three hours later on the chance of finding Mr. Carrados in. Disappointed in this, he had left a note. Carrados cut open the envelope and ran a finger along the following words:—

"Dear Sir,—I have to-day consulted Mr. Louis Carlyle, who thinks that you would like to see me. I will call again in the morning, say at nine o'clock. If this is too soon or otherwise inconvenient I entreat you to leave a message fixing as early an hour as possible.

"Yours faithfully,

"Herbert Draycott.

"P.S.—I should add that I am the renter of a safe at the Lucas Street depository. H.D."

A description of Mr. Draycott made it clear that he was not the West-End bookmaker. The caller, the servant explained, was a thin, wiry, keen-faced man. Carrados felt agreeably interested in this development, which seemed to justify his suspicion of a plot.

At five minutes to nine the next morning Mr. Draycott again presented himself.

"Very good of you to see me so soon, sir," he apologized, on Carrados at once receiving him. "I don't know much of English ways—I'm an Australian—and I was afraid it might be too early."

"You could have made it a couple of hours earlier as far as I am concerned," replied Carrados. "Or you either for that matter, I imagine," he added, "for I don't think that you slept much last night."

"I didn't sleep at all last night," corrected Mr. Draycott. "But it's strange that you should have seen that. I understood from Mr. Carlyle that you—excuse me if I am mistaken, sir—but I understood that you were blind."

Carrados laughed his admission lightly.

"Oh yes," he said. "But never mind that. What is the trouble?"

"I'm afraid it means more than just trouble for me, Mr. Carrados." The man had steady, half-closed eyes, with the suggestion of depth which one notices in the eyes of those whose business it is to look out over great expanses of land or water; they were turned towards Carrados's face with quiet resignation in their frankness now. "I'm afraid it spells disaster. I am a working engineer from the Mount Magdalena district of Coolgardie. I don't want to take up your time with outside details, so I will only say that about two years ago I had an opportunity of acquiring a share in a very promising claim—gold, you understand, both reef and alluvial. As the work went on I put more and more into the undertaking—you couldn't call it a venture by that time. The results were good, better than we had dared to expect, but from one cause and another the expenses were terrible. We saw that it was a bigger thing than we had bargained for and we admitted that we must get outside help."

So far Mr. Draycott's narrative had proceeded smoothly enough under the influence of the quiet despair that had come over the man. But at this point a sudden recollection of his position swept him into a frenzy of bitterness.

"Oh, what the blazes is the good of going over all this again!" he broke out. "What can you or anyone else do anyhow? I've been robbed, rooked, cleared out of everything I possess," and tormented by recollections and by the impotence of his rage the unfortunate engineer beat the oak table with the back of his hand until his knuckles bled.

Carrados waited until the fury had passed.

"Continue, if you please, Mr. Draycott," he said. "Just what you thought it best to tell me is just what I want to know."

"I'm sorry, sir," apologized the man, colouring under his tanned skin. "I ought to be able to control myself better. But this business has shaken me. Three times last night I looked down the barrel of my revolver, and three times I threw it away.... Well, we arranged that I should come to London to interest some financiers in the property. We might have done it locally or in Perth, to be sure, but then, don't you see, they would have wanted to get control. Six weeks ago I landed here. I brought with me specimens of the quartz and good samples of extracted gold, dust and nuggets, the clearing up of several weeks' working, about two hundred and forty ounces in all. That includes the Magdalena Lodestar, our lucky nugget, a lump weighing just under seven pounds of pure gold.

"I had seen an advertisement of this Lucas Street safe-deposit and it seemed just the thing I wanted. Besides the gold, I had all the papers to do with the claims—plans, reports, receipts, licences and so on. Then when I cashed my letter of credit I had about one hundred and fifty pounds in notes. Of course I could have left everything at a bank, but it was more convenient to have it, as it were, in my own safe, to get at any time, and to have a private room that I could take any gentlemen to. I hadn't a suspicion that anything could be wrong. Negotiations hung on in several quarters—it's a bad time to do business here, I find. Then, yesterday, I wanted something. I went to Lucas Street, as I had done half-a-dozen times before, opened my safe, and had the inner case carried to a room.... Mr. Carrados, it was empty!"

"Quite empty?"

"No." He laughed bitterly. "At the bottom was a sheet of wrapper paper. I recognized it as a piece I had left there in case I wanted to make up a parcel. But for that I should have been convinced that I had somehow opened the wrong safe. That was my first idea."

"It cannot be done."

"So I understand, sir. And, then, there was the paper with my name written on it in the empty tin. I was dazed; it seemed impossible. I think I stood there without moving for minutes—it was more like hours. Then I closed the tin box again, took it back, locked up the safe and came out."

"Without notifying anything wrong?"

"Yes, Mr. Carrados." The steady blue eyes regarded him with pained thoughtfulness. "You see, I reckoned it out in that time that it must be someone about the place who had done it."

"You were wrong," said Carrados.

"So Mr. Carlyle seemed to think. I only knew that the key had never been out of my possession and I had told no one of the password. Well, it did come over me rather like cold water down the neck, that there was I alone in the strongest dungeon in London and not a living soul knew where I was."

"Possibly a sort of up-to-date Sweeney Todd's?"

"I'd heard of such things in London," admitted Draycott. "Anyway, I got out. It was a mistake; I see it now. Who is to believe me as it is—it sounds a sort of unlikely tale. And how do they come to pick on me? to know what I had? I don't drink, or open my mouth, or hell round. It beats me."

"They didn't pick on you—you picked on them," replied Carrados. "Never mind how; you'll be believed all right. But as for getting anything back—" The unfinished sentence confirmed Mr. Draycott in his gloomiest anticipations.

"I have the numbers of the notes," he suggested, with an attempt at hopefulness. "They can be stopped, I take it?"

"Stopped? Yes," admitted Carrados. "And what does that amount to? The banks and the police stations will be notified and every little public-house between here and Land's End will change one for the scribbling of 'John Jones' across the back. No, Mr. Draycott, it's awkward, I dare say, but you must make up your mind to wait until you can get fresh supplies from home. Where are you staying?"

Draycott hesitated.

"I have been at the Abbotsford, in Bloomsbury, up to now," he said, with some embarrassment. "The fact is, Mr. Carrados, I think I ought to have told you how I was placed before consulting you, because I—I see no prospect of being able to pay my way. Knowing that I had plenty in the safe, I had run it rather close. I went chiefly yesterday to get some notes. I have a week's hotel bill in my pocket, and"—he glanced down at his trousers—"I've ordered one or two other things unfortunately."

"That will be a matter of time, doubtless," suggested the other encouragingly.

Instead of replying Draycott suddenly dropped his arms on to the table and buried his face between them. A minute passed in silence.

"It's no good, Mr. Carrados," he said, when he was able to speak. "I can't meet it. Say what you like, I simply can't tell those chaps that I've lost everything we had and ask them to send me more. They couldn't do it if I did. Understand sir. The mine is a valuable one; we have the greatest faith in it, but it has gone beyond our depth. The three of us have put everything we own into it. While I am here they are doing labourers' work for a wage, just to keep going ... waiting, oh, my God! waiting for good news from me!"

Carrados walked round the table to his desk and wrote. Then, without a word, he held out a paper to his visitor.

"What's this?" demanded Draycott, in bewilderment. "It's—it's a cheque for a hundred pounds."

"It will carry you on," explained Carrados imperturbably. "A man like you isn't going to throw up the sponge for this set-back. Cable to your partners that you require copies of all the papers at once. They'll manage it, never fear. The gold ... must go. Write fully by the next mail. Tell them everything and add that in spite of all you feel that you are nearer success than ever."

Mr. Draycott folded the cheque with thoughtful deliberation and put it carefully away in his pocket-book.

"I don't know whether you've guessed as much, sir," he said in a queer voice, "but I think that you've saved a man's life to-day. It's not the money, it's the encouragement ... and faith. If you could see you'd know better than I can say how I feel about it."

Carrados laughed quietly. It always amused him to have people explain how much more he would learn if he had eyes.

"Then we'll go on to Lucas Street and give the manager the shock of his life," was all he said. "Come, Mr. Draycott, I have already rung up the car."

But, as it happened, another instrument had been destined to apply that stimulating experience to the manager. As they stepped out of the car opposite "The Safe" a taxicab drew up and Mr. Carlyle's alert and cheery voice hailed them.

"A moment, Max," he called, turning to settle with his driver, a transaction that he invested with an air of dignified urbanity which almost made up for any small pecuniary disappointment that may have accompanied it. "This is indeed fortunate. Let us compare notes for a moment. I have just received an almost imploring message from the manager to come at once. I assumed that it was the affair of our colonial friend here, but he went on to mention Professor Holmfast Bulge. Can it really be possible that he also has made a similar discovery?"

"What did the manager say?" asked Carrados.

"He was practically incoherent, but I really think it must be so. What have you done?"

"Nothing," replied Carrados. He turned his back on "The Safe" and appeared to be regarding the other side of the street. "There is a tobacconist's shop directly opposite?"

"There is."

"What do they sell on the first floor?"

"Possibly they sell 'Rubbo.' I hazard the suggestion from the legend 'Rub in Rubbo for Everything' which embellishes each window."

"The windows are frosted?"

"They are, to half-way up, mysterious man."

Carrados walked back to his motor-car.

"While we are away, Parkinson, go across and buy a tin, bottle, box or packet of 'Rubbo.'"

"What is 'Rubbo,' Max?" chirped Mr. Carlyle with insatiable curiosity.

"So far we do not know. When Parkinson gets some, Louis, you shall be the one to try it."

They descended into the basement and were passed in by the grille-keeper, whose manner betrayed a discreet consciousness of something in the air. It was unnecessary to speculate why. In the distance, muffled by the armoured passages, an authoritative voice boomed like a sonorous bell heard under water.

"What, however, are the facts?" it was demanding, with the causticity of baffled helplessness. "I am assured that there is no other key in existence; yet my safe has been unlocked. I am given to understand that without the password it would be impossible for an unauthorized person to tamper with my property. My password, deliberately chosen, is 'anthropophaginian,' sir. Is it one that is familiarly on the lips of the criminal classes? But my safe is empty! What is the explanation? Who are the guilty persons? What is being done? Where are the police?"

"If you consider that the proper course to adopt is to stand on the doorstep and beckon in the first constable who happens to pass, permit me to say, sir, that I differ from you," retorted the distracted manager. "You may rely on everything possible being done to clear up the mystery. As I told you, I have already telephoned for a capable private detective and for one of my directors."

"But that is not enough," insisted the professor angrily. "Will one mere private detective restore my £6000 Japanese 4-1/2 per cent. bearer bonds? Is the return of my irreplaceable notes on 'Polyphyletic Bridal Customs among the mid-Pleistocene Cave Men' to depend on a solitary director? I demand that the police shall be called in—as many as are available. Let Scotland Yard be set in motion. A searching inquiry must be made. I have only been a user of your precious establishment for six months, and this is the result."

"There you hold the key of the mystery, Professor Bulge," interposed Carrados quietly.

"Who is this, sir?" demanded the exasperated professor at large.

"Permit me," explained Mr. Carlyle, with bland assurance. "I am Louis Carlyle, of Bampton Street. This gentleman is Mr. Max Carrados, the eminent amateur specialist in crime."

"I shall be thankful for any assistance towards elucidating this appalling business," condescended the professor sonorously. "Let me put you in possession of the facts—"

"Perhaps if we went into your room," suggested Carrados to the manager, "we should be less liable to interruption."

"Quite so; quite so," boomed the professor, accepting the proposal on everyone else's behalf. "The facts, sir, are these: I am the unfortunate possessor of a safe here, in which, a few months ago, I deposited—among less important matter—sixty bearer bonds of the Japanese Imperial Loan—the bulk of my small fortune—and the manuscript of an important projected work on 'Polyphyletic Bridal Customs among the mid-Pleistocene Cave Men.' Today I came to detach the coupons which fall due on the fifteenth; to pay them into my bank a week in advance, in accordance with my custom. What do I find? I find the safe locked and apparently intact, as when I last saw it a month ago. But it is far from being intact, sir! It has been opened, ransacked, cleared out! Not a single bond, not a scrap of paper remains."

It was obvious that the manager's temperature had been rising during the latter part of this speech and now he boiled over.

"Pardon my flatly contradicting you, Professor Bulge. You have again referred to your visit here a month ago as your last. You will bear witness of that, gentlemen. When I inform you that the professor had access to his safe as recently as on Monday last you will recognize the importance that the statement may assume."

The professor glared across the room like an infuriated animal, a comparison heightened by his notoriously hircine appearance.

"How dare you contradict me, sir!" he cried, slapping the table sharply with his open hand. "I was not here on Monday."

The manager shrugged his shoulders coldly.

"You forget that the attendants also saw you," he remarked. "Cannot we trust our own eyes?"

"A common assumption, yet not always a strictly reliable one," insinuated Carrados softly.

"I cannot be mistaken."

"Then can you tell me, without looking, what colour Professor Bulge's eyes are?"

There was a curious and expectant silence for a minute. The professor turned his back on the manager and the manager passed from thoughtfulness to embarrassment.

"I really do not know, Mr. Carrados," he declared loftily at last. "I do not refer to mere trifles like that."

"Then you can be mistaken," replied Carrados mildly yet with decision.

"But the ample hair, the venerable flowing beard, the prominent nose and heavy eyebrows—"

"These are just the striking points that are most easily counterfeited. They 'take the eye.' If you would ensure yourself against deception, learn rather to observe the eye itself, and particularly the spots on it, the shape of the finger-nails, the set of the ears. These things cannot be simulated."

"You seriously suggest that the man was not Professor Bulge—that he was an impostor?"

"The conclusion is inevitable. Where were you on Monday, Professor?"

"I was on a short lecturing tour in the Midlands. On Saturday I was in Nottingham. On Monday in Birmingham. I did not return to London until yesterday."

Carrados turned to the manager again and indicated Draycott, who so far had remained in the background.

"And this gentleman? Did he by any chance come here on Monday?"

"He did not, Mr. Carrados. But I gave him access to his safe on Tuesday afternoon and again yesterday."

Draycott shook his head sadly.

"Yesterday I found it empty," he said. "And all Tuesday afternoon I was at Brighton, trying to see a gentleman on business."

The manager sat down very suddenly.

"Good God, another!" he exclaimed faintly.

"I am afraid the list is only beginning," said Carrados. "We must go through your renters' book."

The manager roused himself to protest.

"That cannot be done. No one but myself or my deputy ever sees the book. It would be— unprecedented."

"The circumstances are unprecedented," replied Carrados.

"If any difficulties are placed in the way of these gentlemen's investigations, I shall make it my duty to bring the facts before the Home Secretary," announced the professor, speaking up to the ceiling with the voice of a brazen trumpet.

Carrados raised a deprecating hand.

"May I make a suggestion?" he remarked. "Now, I am blind. If, therefore—?"

"Very well," acquiesced the manager. "But I must request the others to withdraw."

For five minutes Carrados followed the list of safe-renters as the manager read them to him. Sometimes he stopped the catalogue to reflect a moment; now and then he brushed a finger-tip over a written signature and compared it with another. Occasionally a password interested him. But when the list came to an end he continued to look into space without any sign of enlightenment.

"So much is perfectly clear and yet so much is incredible," he mused. "You insist that you alone have been in charge for the last six months?"

"I have not been away a day this year."

"Meals?"

"I have my lunch sent in."

"And this room could not be entered without your knowledge while you were about the place?"

"It is impossible. The door is fitted with a powerful spring and a feather-touch self-acting lock. It cannot be left unlocked unless you deliberately prop it open."

"And, with your knowledge, no one has had an opportunity of having access to this book?"

"No," was the reply.

Carrados stood up and began to put on his gloves.

"Then I must decline to pursue my investigation any further," he said icily.

"Why?" stammered the manager.

"Because I have positive reason for believing that you are deceiving me."

"Pray sit down, Mr. Carrados. It is quite true that when you put the last question to me a circumstance rushed into my mind which—so far as the strict letter was concerned—might seem to demand 'Yes' instead of 'No.' But not in the spirit of your inquiry. It would be absurd to attach any importance to the incident I refer to."

"That would be for me to judge."

"You shall do so, Mr. Carrados. I live at Windermere Mansions with my sister. A few months ago she got to know a married couple who had recently come to the opposite flat. The husband was a middle-aged, scholarly man who spent most of his time in the British Museum. His wife's tastes were different; she was much younger, brighter, gayer; a mere girl in fact, one of the most charming and unaffected I have ever met. My sister Amelia does not readily—"

"Stop!" exclaimed Carrados. "A studious middle-aged man and a charming young wife! Be as brief as possible. If there is any chance it may turn on a matter of minutes at the ports. She came here, of course?"

"Accompanied by her husband," replied the manager stiffly. "Mrs. Scott had travelled and she had a hobby of taking photographs wherever she went. When my position accidentally came out one evening she was carried away by the novel idea of adding views of a safe deposit to her collection—as enthusiastic as a child. There was no reason why she should not; the place has often been taken for advertising purposes."

"She came, and brought her camera—under your very nose!"

"I do not know what you mean by 'under my very nose.' She came with her husband one evening just about closing time. She brought her camera, of course—quite a small affair."

"And contrived to be in here alone?"

"I take exception to the word 'contrived.' It—it happened. I sent out for some tea, and in the course—"

"How long was she alone in here?"

"Two or three minutes at the most. When I returned she was seated at my desk. That was what I referred to. The little rogue had put on my glasses and had got hold of a big book. We were great chums, and she delighted to mock me. I confess that I was startled—merely instinctively—to see that she had taken up this book, but the next moment I saw that she had it upside down."

"Clever! She couldn't get it away in time. And the camera, with half-a-dozen of its specially sensitized films already snapped over the last few pages, by her side!"

"That child!"

"Yes. She is twenty-seven and has kicked hats off tall men's heads in every capital from Petersburg to Buenos Ayres! Get through to Scotland Yard and ask if Inspector Beedel can come up."

The manager breathed heavily through his nose.

"To call in the police and publish everything would ruin this establishment—confidence would be gone. I cannot do it without further authority."

"Then the professor certainly will."

"Before you came I rang up the only director who is at present in town and gave him the facts as they then stood. Possibly he has arrived by this. If you will accompany me to the boardroom we will see."

They went up to the floor above, Mr. Carlyle joining them on the way.

"Excuse me a moment," said the manager.

Parkinson, who had been having an improving conversation with the hall porter on the subject of land values, approached.

"I am sorry, sir," he reported, "but I was unable to procure any 'Rubbo.' The place appears to be shut up."

"That is a pity; Mr. Carlyle had set his heart on it."

"Will you come this way, please?" said the manager, reappearing.

In the boardroom they found a white-haired old gentleman who had obeyed the manager's behest from a sense of duty, and then remained in a distant corner of the empty room in the hope that he might be over-looked. He was amiably helpless and appeared to be deeply aware of it.

"This is a very sad business, gentlemen," he said, in a whispering, confiding voice. "I am informed that you recommend calling in the Scotland Yard authorities. That would be a disastrous course for an institution that depends on the implicit confidence of the public."

"It is the only course," replied Carrados.

"The name of Mr. Carrados is well known to us in connection with a delicate case. Could you not carry this one through?"

"It is impossible. A wide inquiry must be made. Every port will have to be watched. The police alone can do that." He threw a little significance into the next sentence. "I alone can put the police in the right way of doing it."

"And you will do that, Mr. Carrados?"

Carrados smiled engagingly. He knew exactly what constituted the great attraction of his services.

"My position is this," he explained. "So far my work has been entirely amateur. In that capacity I have averted one or two crimes, remedied an occasional injustice, and now and then been of service to my professional friend, Louis Carlyle. But there is no reason at all why I should serve a commercial firm in an ordinary affair of business for nothing. For any information I should require a fee, a quite nominal fee of, say, one hundred pounds."

The director looked as though his faith in human nature had received a rude blow.

"A hundred pounds would be a very large initial fee for a small firm like this, Mr. Carrados," he remarked in a pained voice.

"And that, of course, would be independent of Mr. Carlyle's professional charges," added Carrados.

"Is that sum contingent on any specific performance?" inquired the manager.

"I do not mind making it conditional on my procuring for you, for the police to act on, a photograph and a description of the thief."

The two officials conferred apart for a moment. Then the manager returned.

"We will agree, Mr. Carrados, on the understanding that these things are to be in our hands within two days. Failing that—"

"No, no!" cried Mr. Carlyle indignantly, but Carrados good-humouredly put him aside.

"I will accept the condition in the same sporting spirit that inspires it. Within forty-eight hours or no pay. The cheque, of course, to be given immediately the goods are delivered?"

"You may rely on that."

Carrados took out his pocket-book, produced an envelope bearing an American stamp, and from it extracted an unmounted print.

"Here is the photograph," he announced. "The man is called Ulysses K. Groom, but he is better known as 'Harry the Actor.' You will find the description written on the back."

Five minutes later, when they were alone, Mr. Carlyle expressed his opinion of the transaction.

"You are an unmitigated humbug, Max," he said, "though an amiable one, I admit. But purely for your own private amusement you spring these things on people."

"On the contrary," replied Carrados, "people spring these things on me."

"Now this photograph. Why have I heard nothing of it before?"

Carrados took out his watch and touched the fingers.

"It is now three minutes to eleven. I received the photograph at twenty past eight."

"Even then, an hour ago you assured me that you had done nothing."

"Nor had I—so far as result went. Until the keystone of the edifice was wrung from the manager in his room, I was as far away from demonstrable certainty as ever."

"So am I—as yet," hinted Mr. Carlyle.

"I am coming to that, Louis. I turn over the whole thing to you. The man has got two clear days' start and the chances are nine to one against catching him. We know everything, and the case has no further interest for me. But it is your business. Here is your material.

"On that one occasion when the 'tawny' man crossed our path, I took from the first a rather more serious view of his scope and intention than you did. The same day I sent a cipher cable to Pierson of the New York service. I asked for news of any man of such and such a description—merely negative—who was known to have left the States; an educated man, expert in the use of disguises, audacious in his operations, and a specialist in 'dry' work among banks and strong-rooms."

"Why the States, Max?"

"That was a sighting shot on my part. I argued that he must be an English-speaking man. The smart and inventive turn of the modern Yank has made him a specialist in ingenious devices, straight or crooked. Unpickable locks and invincible lock-pickers, burglar-proof safes and safe-specializing burglars, come equally from the States. So I tried a very simple test. As we talked that day and the man walked past us, I dropped the words 'New York'—or, rather, 'Noo Y'rk'—in his hearing."

"I know you did. He neither turned nor stopped."

"He was that much on his guard; but into his step there came—though your poor old eyes could not see it, Louis—the 'psychological pause,' an absolute arrest of perhaps a fifth of a second; just as it would have done with you if the word 'London' had fallen on your ear in a distant land. However, the whys and the wherefores don't matter. Here is the essential story.

"Eighteen months ago 'Harry the Actor' successfully looted the office safe of M'Kenkie, J.F. Higgs & Co., of Cleveland, Ohio. He had just married a smart but very facile third-rate vaudeville actress—English by origin—and wanted money for the honeymoon. He got about five hundred pounds, and with that they came to Europe and stayed in London for some months. That period is marked by the Congreave Square post office burglary, you may remember. While studying such of the British institutions as most appealed to him, the 'Actor's' attention became fixed on this safe-deposit. Possibly the implied challenge contained in its telegraphic address grew on him until it became a point of professional honour with him to despoil it; at all events he was presumably attracted by an undertaking that promised not only glory but very solid profit. The first part of the plot was, to the most skilful criminal 'impersonator' in the States, mere skittles. Spreading over those months he appeared at 'The Safe' in twelve different characters and rented twelve safes of different sizes. At the same time he made a thorough study of the methods of the place. As soon as possible he got the keys back again into legitimate use, having made duplicates for his own private ends, of course. Five he seems to have returned during his first stay; one was received later, with profuse apologies, by registered post; one was returned through a leading Berlin bank. Six months ago he made a flying visit here, purely to work off two more. One he kept from first to last, and the remaining couple he got in at the beginning of his second long residence here, three or four months ago.

"This brings us to the serious part of the cool enterprise. He had funds from the Atlantic and South-Central Mail-car coup when he arrived here last April. He appears to have set up three establishments; a home, in the guise of an elderly scholar with a young wife, which, of course, was next door to our friend the manager; an observation point, over which he plastered the inscription 'Rub in Rubbo for Everything' as a reason for being; and, somewhere else, a dressing-room with essential conditions of two doors into different streets.

"About six weeks ago he entered the last stage. Mrs. Harry, with quite ridiculous ease, got photographs of the necessary page or two of the record-book. I don't doubt that for weeks before then everyone who entered the place had been observed, but the photographs linked them up with the actual men into whose hands the 'Actor's' old keys had passed—gave their names and addresses, the numbers of their safes, their passwords and signatures. The rest was easy."

"Yes, by Jupiter; mere play for a man like that," agreed Mr. Carlyle, with professional admiration. "He could contrive a dozen different occasions for studying the voice and manner and appearance of his victims. How much has he cleared?"

"We can only speculate as yet. I have put my hand on seven doubtful callers on Monday and Tuesday last. Two others he had ignored for some reason; the remaining two safes had not been allotted. There is one point that raises an interesting speculation."

"What is that, Max?"

"The 'Actor' has one associate, a man known as 'Billy the Fondant,' but beyond that—with the exception of his wife, of course—he does not usually trust anyone. It is plain, however, that at least seven men must latterly have been kept under close observation. It has occurred to me—"

"Yes, Max?"

"I have wondered whether Harry has enlisted the innocent services of one or other of our private inquiry offices."

"Scarcely," smiled the professional. "It would hardly pass muster."

"Oh, I don't know. Mrs. Harry, in the character of a jealous wife or a suspicious sweetheart, might reasonably—"

Mr. Carlyle's smile suddenly faded.

"By Jupiter!" he exclaimed. "I remember—"

"Yes, Louis?" prompted Carrados, with laughter in his voice.

"I remember that I must telephone to a client before Beedel comes," concluded Mr. Carlyle, rising in some haste.

At the door he almost ran into the subdued director, who was wringing his hands in helpless protest at a new stroke of calamity.

"Mr. Carrados," wailed the poor old gentleman in a tremulous bleat, "Mr. Carrados, there is another now—Sir Benjamin Gump. He insists on seeing me. You will not—you will not desert us?"

"I should have to stay a week," replied Carrados briskly, "and I'm just off now. There will be a procession. Mr. Carlyle will support you, I am sure."

He nodded "Good-morning" straight into the eyes of each and found his way out with the astonishing certainty of movement that made so many forget his infirmity. Possibly he was not desirous of encountering Draycott's embarrassed gratitude again, for in less than a minute they heard the swirl of his departing car.

"Never mind, my dear sir," Mr. Carlyle assured his client, with impenetrable complacency. "Never mind. I will remain instead. Perhaps I had better make myself known to Sir Benjamin at once."

The director turned on him the pleading, trustful look of a cornered dormouse.

"He is in the basement," he whispered. "I shall be in the boardroom—if necessary."

Mr. Carlyle had no difficulty in discovering the centre of interest in the basement. Sir Benjamin was expansive and reserved, bewildered and decisive, long-winded and short-tempered, each in turn and more or less all at once. He had already demanded the attention of the manager, Professor Bulge, Draycott and two underlings to his case and they were now involved in a babel of inutile reiteration. The inquiry agent was at once drawn into a circle of interrogation that he did his best to satisfy impressively while himself learning the new facts.

The latest development was sufficiently astonishing. Less than an hour before Sir Benjamin had received a parcel by district messenger. It contained a jewel-case which ought at that moment to have been securely reposing in one of the deposit safes. Hastily snatching it open, the recipient's incredible forebodings were realized. It was empty—empty of jewels, that is to say, for, as if to add a sting to the blow, a neatly inscribed card had been placed inside, and on it the agitated baronet read the appropriate but at the moment rather gratuitous maxim: "Lay not up for yourselves treasures upon earth—"

The card was passed round and all eyes demanded the expert's pronouncement.

"'—where moth and rust doth corrupt and where thieves break through and steal.' H'm," read Mr. Carlyle with weight. "This is a most important clue, Sir Benjamin—"

"Hey, what? What's that?" exclaimed a voice from the other side of the hall. "Why, damme if I don't believe you've got another! Look at that, gentlemen; look at that. What's on, I say? Here now, come; give me my safe. I want to know where I am."

It was the bookmaker who strode tempestuously in among them, flourishing before their faces a replica of the card that was in Mr. Carlyle's hand.

"Well, upon my soul this is most extraordinary," exclaimed that gentleman, comparing the two. "You have just received this, Mr.—Mr. Berge, isn't it?"

"That's right, Berge—'Iceberg' on the course. Thank the Lord Harry, I can take my losses coolly enough, but this—this is a facer. Put into my hand half-an-hour ago inside an envelope that ought to be here and as safe as in the Bank of England. What's the game, I say? Here, Johnny, hurry and let me into my safe."

Discipline and method had for the moment gone by the board. There was no suggestion of the boasted safeguards of the establishment. The manager added his voice to that of the client, and when the attendant did not at once appear he called again.

"John, come and give Mr. Berge access to his safe at once."

"All right, sir," pleaded the harassed key-attendant, hurrying up with the burden of his own distraction. "There's a silly fathead got in what thinks this is a left-luggage office, so far as I can make out—a foreigner."

"Never mind that now," replied the manager severely, "Mr. Berge's safe: No. 01724."

The attendant and Mr. Berge went off together down one of the brilliant colonnaded vistas. One or two of the others who had caught the words glanced across and became aware of a strange figure that was drifting indecisively towards them. He was obviously an elderly German tourist of pronounced type— long-haired, spectacled, outrageously garbed and involved in the mental abstraction of his philosophical race. One hand was occupied with the manipulation of a pipe, as markedly Teutonic as its owner; the other grasped a carpet-bag that would have ensured an opening laugh to any low comedian.

Quite impervious to the preoccupation of the group, the German made his way up to them and picked out the manager.

"This was a safety deposit, nicht wahr?"

"Quite so," acquiesced the manager loftily, "but just now—"

"Your fellow was dense of comprehension." The eyes behind the clumsy glasses wrinkled to a ponderous humour. "He forgot his own business. Now this goot bag—"

Brought into fuller prominence, the carpet-bag revealed further details of its overburdened proportions. At one end a flannel shirt cuff protruded in limp dejection; at the other an ancient collar, with the grotesque attachment known as a "dickey," asserted its presence. No wonder the manager frowned his annoyance. "The Safe" was in low enough repute among its patrons at that moment without any burlesque interlude to its tragic hour.

"Yes, yes," he whispered, attempting to lead the would-be depositor away, "but you are under a mistake. This is not—"

"It was a safety deposit? Goot. Mine bag—I would deposit him in safety till the time of mine train. Ja?"

"Nein, nein!" almost hissed the agonized official. "Go away, sir, go away! It isn't a cloakroom. John, let this gentleman out."

The attendant and Mr. Berge were returning from their quest. The inner box had been opened and there was no need to ask the result. The bookmaker was shaking his head like a baffled bull.

"Gone, no effects," he shouted across the hall. "Lifted from 'The Safe,' by crumb!"

To those who knew nothing of the method and operation of the fraud it seemed as if the financial security of the Capital was tottering. An amazed silence fell, and in it they heard the great grille door of the basement clang on the inopportune foreigner's departure. But, as if it was impossible to stand still on that morning of dire happenings, he was immediately succeeded by a dapper, keen-faced man in severe clerical attire who had been let in as the intruder passed out.

"Canon Petersham!" exclaimed the professor, going forward to greet him.

"My dear Professor Bulge!" reciprocated the canon. "You here! A most disquieting thing has happened to me. I must have my safe at once." He divided his attention between the manager and the professor as he monopolized them both. "A most disquieting and—and outrageous circumstance. My safe, please— yes, yes, Rev. Henry Noakes Petersham. I have just received by hand a box, a small box of no value but one that I thought, yes, I am convinced that it was the one, a box that was used to contain certain valuables of family interest which should at this moment be in my safe here. No. 7436? Very likely, very likely. Yes, here is my key. But not content with the disconcerting effect of that, professor, the box contained—and I protest that it's a most unseemly thing to quote any text from the Bible in this way to a clergyman of my position—well, here it is. 'Lay not up for yourselves treasures upon earth—' Why, I have a dozen sermons of my own in my desk now on that very verse. I'm particularly partial to the very needful lesson that it teaches. And to apply it to me! It's monstrous!"

"No. 7436, John," ordered the manager, with weary resignation.

The attendant again led the way towards another armour-plated aisle. Smartly turning a corner, he stumbled over something, bit a profane exclamation in two, and looked back.

"It's that bloomin' foreigner's old bag again," he explained across the place in aggrieved apology. "He left it here after all."

"Take it upstairs and throw it out when you've finished," said the manager shortly.

"Here, wait a minute," pondered John, in absent-minded familiarity. "Wait a minute. This is a funny go. There's a label on that wasn't here before. 'Why not look inside?'"

"'Why not look inside?'" repeated someone.

"That's what it says."

There was another puzzled silence. All were arrested by some intangible suggestion of a deeper mystery than they had yet touched. One by one they began to cross the hall with the conscious air of men who were not curious but thought that they might as well see.

"Why, curse my crumpet," suddenly exploded Mr. Berge, "if that ain't the same writing as these texts!"

"By gad, but I believe you are right," assented Mr. Carlyle. "Well, why not look inside?"

The attendant, from his stooping posture, took the verdict of the ring of faces and in a trice tugged open the two buckles. The central fastening was not locked, and yielded to a touch. The flannel shirt, the weird collar and a few other garments in the nature of a "top-dressing" were flung out and John's hand plunged deeper....

Harry the Actor had lived up to his dramatic instinct. Nothing was wrapped up; nay, the rich booty had been deliberately opened out and displayed, as it were, so that the overturning of the bag, when John the keybearer in an access of riotous extravagance lifted it up and strewed its contents broadcast on the floor, was like the looting of a smuggler's den, or the realization of a speculator's dream, or the bursting of an Aladdin's cave, or something incredibly lavish and bizarre. Bank-notes fluttered down and lay about in all directions, relays of sovereigns rolled away like so much dross, bonds and scrip for thousands and tens of thousands clogged the downpouring stream of jewellery and unset gems. A yellow stone the size of a four-pound weight and twice as heavy dropped plump upon the canon's toes and sent him hopping and grimacing to the wall. A ruby-hilted kris cut across the manager's wrist as he strove to arrest the splendid rout. Still the miraculous cornucopia deluged the ground, with its pattering, ringing, bumping, crinkling, rolling, fluttering produce until, like the final tableau of some spectacular ballet, it ended with a golden rain that masked the details of the heap beneath a glittering veil of yellow sand.

"My dust!" gasped Draycott.

"My fivers, by golly!" ejaculated the bookmaker, initiating a plunge among the spoil.

"My Japanese bonds, coupons and all, and—yes, even the manuscript of my work on 'Polyphyletic Bridal Customs among the mid-Pleistocene Cave Men.' Hah!" Something approaching a cachinnation of delight closed the professor's contribution to the pandemonium, and eyewitnesses afterwards declared that for a moment the dignified scientist stood on one foot in the opening movement of a can-can.

"My wife's diamonds, thank heaven!" cried Sir Benjamin, with the air of a schoolboy who was very well out of a swishing.

"But what does it mean?" demanded the bewildered canon. "Here are my family heirlooms—a few decent pearls, my grandfather's collection of camei and other trifles—but who—?"

"Perhaps this offers some explanation," suggested Mr. Carlyle, unpinning an envelope that had been secured to the lining of the bag. "It is addressed 'To Seven Rich Sinners.' Shall I read it for you?"

For some reason the response was not unanimous, but it was sufficient. Mr. Carlyle cut open the envelope.

"My dear Friends,—Aren't you glad? Aren't you happy at this moment? Ah yes; but not with the true joy of regeneration that alone can bring lightness to the afflicted soul. Pause while there is yet time. Cast off the burden of your sinful lusts, for what shall it profit a man if he shall gain the whole world and lose his own soul? (Mark, chap. viii, v. 36.)

"Oh, my friends, you have had an all-fired narrow squeak. Up till the Friday in last week I held your wealth in the hollow of my ungodly hand and rejoiced in my nefarious cunning, but on that day as I with my guilty female accomplice stood listening with worldly amusement to the testimony of a converted brother at a meeting of the Salvation Army on Clapham Common, the gospel light suddenly shone into our rebellious souls and then and there we found salvation. Hallelujah!

"What we have done to complete the unrighteous scheme upon which we had laboured for months has only been for your own good, dear friends that you are, though as yet divided from us by your carnal lusts. Let this be a lesson to you. Sell all you have and give it to the poor—through the organization of the Salvation Army by preference—and thereby lay up for yourselves treasures where neither moth nor rust doth corrupt and where thieves do not break through and steal. (Matthew, chap. vi, v. 20.)

"Yours in good works,
Private Henry, the Salvationist.

"P.S. (in haste).—I may as well inform you that no crib is really uncrackable, though the Cyrus J. Coy Co.'s Safe Deposit on West 24th Street, N.Y., comes nearest the kernel. And even that I could work to the bare rock if I took hold of the job with both hands—that is to say I could have done in my sinful days. As for you, I should recommend you to change your T.A. to 'Peanut.'

"U.K.G."

"There sounds a streak of the old Adam in that postscript, Mr. Carlyle," whispered Inspector Beedel, who had just arrived in time to hear the letter read.

Ernest Bramah – A Concise Bibliography

Kai Lung Series

The Wallet of Kai Lung (1900)
Kai Lung's Golden Hours (1922)
Kai Lung Unrolls His Mat (1928)

The Moon of Much Gladness (1932; published in the United States as The return of Kai Lung)
The Kai Lung Omnibus (1936) (The Wallet of Kai Lung/Kai Lung's Golden Hours/Kai Lung Unrolls His Mat
Kai Lung Beneath the Mulberry Tree (1940)
The Celestial Omnibus (1940; selected stories from the earlier books)

Max Carrados Series

Books
Max Carrados (1914)
The Eyes of Max Carrados (1923)
Max Carrados Mysteries (1927)
The Bravo of London (1934)

Short Stories
The Master Coiner Unmasked. 17 August 1913.
The Mystery of the Signals. 24 and 31 August 1913.
The Tragedy at Brookbend Cottage. 7 and 14 September 1913.
The Clever Mrs Straithwaite. 21 and 28 September 1913.
The Great Safe Deposit Coup. 5 and 12 October 1913.
The Tilling Shaw Mystery. 19 and 26 October 1913.
The Secret of Dunstan's Tower. 2 and 9 November 1913.
The Comedy at Fountain Cottage. 16 and 23 November 1913.
The Kingsmouth German Spy Case. 30 November and 7 December 1913.
The Missing Actress Sensation. 14 December 1913.
The Virginiola Fraud. 21 December 1913.
The Game Played in the Dark. 28 December 1913.
The Bunch of Violets. Strand Magazine, July 1924.
The Disappearance of Marie Severe. Apparently first published in The Eyes of Max Carrados
The Mystery of the Poisoned Dish of Mushrooms. Apparently first published in The Eyes of Max Carrados
The Ghost at Massingham Mansions. Apparently first published in The Eyes of Max Carrados
The Ingenious Mr Spinola. Apparently first published in The Eyes of Max Carrados
The Eastern Mystery. Apparently first published in The Eyes of Max Carrados
The Secret of Headlam Heights. Apparently first published in Max Carrados Mysteries
The Vanished Crown. Apparently first published in Max Carrados Mysteries
The Holloway Flat Tragedy. Apparently first published in Max Carrados Mysteries
The Curious Circumstances of the Two Left Shoes. Apparently first published in Max Carrados Mysteries
The Ingenious Mind of Mr Rigby Lacksome. Apparently first published in Max Carrados Mysteries
The Crime at the House in Culver Street. Apparently first published in Max Carrados Mysteries
The Strange Case of Cyril Bycourt. Apparently first published in Max Carrados Mysteries
The Missing Witness Sensation. July 1926

Plays
Blind Man's Bluff. (1918). Collected in Bodies from the Library (Ed. Tony Medawar)

Adaptations by Others
In the Dark (1917) - Gilbert Heron

Other fiction

Books

The Mirror of Kong Ho (1905)
The Secret of the League (1907)
The Specimen Case (1924) (Includes a Kai Lung story and a Max Carrados story, The Bunch of Violets)
Short Stories of To-day and Yesterday (1929). Includes eleven stories by Bramah
A Little Flutter (1930)

Short Stories

The Story of Young Chang. October 1896
The Story of Kin-Yen, the Picture-Maker. December 1898
The Duplicity of Tiao. December 1900
The Impiety of Yuan Yan. February 1904
The Dragon of Swafton. July 1904
The Goose and the Golden Egg. February 1907
The War Hawks. September 1909
The Great Hockington Find. February 1910
The Red Splinter. April 1913
The Chief Examiner. 1914
The Story of Kin Weng and the Miraculous Tusk. June 1927
The Ill-Regulated Destiny of Kin Yeng, the Picture-Maker. A two-part story. August 1938

Nonfiction

Books

English Farming and Why I Turned It Up (1894)
A Guide to the Varieties and Rarity of English Regal Copper Coins, Charles II-Victoria, 1671–1860 (1929)
A Handbook for Writers and Artists: a practical guide for contributors to the press and to literary and artistic publications; by a London editor [i.e. E. B. Smith]. London: Charles William Deacon & Co., 1898

Short Pieces

While You Wait. The Bystander, December 1905